The Wanted Shorts

Blind Love
This Love
Reckless Love
*Series available on audiobook

Boston Love Series
Searching for Harmony
Fighting for Love
*Series available on audiobook

Austin Singles Series
Seduce Me
Entice Me
Adore Me
*Series available on audiobook

Wanted Series
*Wanted**
*Saved**
*Faithful**
Believe
*Cherished**
*A Forever Love**
The Wanted Short Stories
All They Wanted
*Available on audiobook

Love Wanted in Texas Series
Spin-off series to the WANTED Series
Without You
Saving You
Holding You
Finding You
Chasing You

Loving You
Entire series available on audiobook
*Please note *Loving You* combines the last book of the Broken
and Love Wanted in Texas series.

Broken Series
*Broken**
*Broken Dreams**
*Broken Promises**
Broken Love
*Available on audiobook

The Journey of Love Series
Unconditional Love
Undeniable Love
Unforgettable Love
*Entire series available on audiobook

With Me Series
Stay With Me
Only With Me
*Series available on audiobook

Speed Series
Ignite
Adrenaline
*Series available on audiobook

COLLABORATIONS
Predestined Hearts (co-written with Kristin Mayer)*
*Play Me (*co-written with Kristin Mayer)*
*Dangerous Temptations (*co-written with Kristin Mayer*
*Available on audiobook

The Wanted Shorts

NEW YORK TIMES & USA TODAY BESTSELLING AUTHOR

KELLY ELLIOTT

Wanted

BOOK ONE IN THE WANTED SERIES
SHORT STORY

Chapter One

Ellie

I STOOD AT the kitchen sink, rinsing off vegetables, as I listened to Alex and Colt fighting—again. Alex had just turned nine, and she was well on her way to twenty-one. Colt would be eight in a few months, and he lived to torment his sister.

The phone rang, and I leaned over to pick it up. I was hoping it would be Gunner. He'd taken a job designing a lawyer's new house in Fredericksburg. It was a favor to the architecture firm where he'd worked part-time after college.

"Hello?"

"I need a drink—a tall drink filled with alcohol—preferably served by my naked husband."

I rolled my eyes. "Ew...really? Come on, Ari. No matter how many times I tell you that grosses me out, you just never stop."

I could picture her sitting at her desk with her feet propped up, smiling her devilish smile.

"Tell me you don't feel the same way...well, not about my husband serving the drink to you. Instead, it would be your cowboy."

I closed my eyes and tried to picture it. "That would be heaven, especially since I hardly see him anymore."

"That sucks, sweets. With as busy as the ranch is, I'm surprised he took this job."

I frowned and glanced back to the kids since they had been way too quiet.

"Oh my God, Ari, if you hear me scream, don't panic. I'm fixin' to pull my hair out. I'll call ya right back." I hung up the phone and walked over to the table.

I looked down at Alex. "What did you do?"

I peeked over to Colt. Alex smiled and shrugged her shoulders as she sat down in the chair. She gently laid the scissors on the kitchen table and attempted not to laugh.

I turned back to look at my baby boy. I tried really hard not to laugh, and I bit the inside of my cheek. "Colt, why did you let your sister cut your hair?"

I glanced at Alex. "And is that a wash-out dye, Alexandra?"

She shook her head. "Nope."

Colt jumped up. "You said it would wash out, Alex! You promised it would." He looked at me. "Did she cut my hair good, Mama? She told me she's been practicing on her Barbie dolls."

I placed my fingertips on my temples and silently prayed for a miracle. I wanted the last five minutes to be erased, so I could get a do-over.

I let out a long and dragged-out sigh. "Alex, how in the heck did you find the time to dye his hair and cut it while I was on a three-minute phone call?"

Again, she shrugged her shoulders. "I've learned to move fast, Mama. I have to with Luke and Will."

My mouth dropped open. I shook my head to clear my thoughts. I pointed to the door and said, "Go up to your room, Alex. You're grounded."

"What?" Alex said as she jumped up. "But, Mama, he was being so annoying. He wouldn't stop talking. I had to do something."

"So, you cut chunks of his hair out and dyed the rest?"

"Chunks?" Colt said with a concerned look on his face.

"I said, go to your room, Alex. Your father will deal with your punishment when he gets home because I'm too angry right now."

"Mama, did you say...chunks?" Colt asked.

Alex turned and stormed off.

I looked down at poor Colt. "Baby, can you go into Mommy and Daddy's shower and wash your hair like a big boy?"

He smiled big. "Sure, I can."

As Colt headed off to our bedroom, I walked back over and picked up the phone. I was about to call Ari back when I decided to call my mother instead.

"Hello?"

"Mom?"

"Ellie, darling, how are you?"

I was about to answer her when Colt let out the girliest scream I'd ever heard.

"My hair!" he yelled over and over.

"Are you off work, Mom?" I said as tears formed in my eyes.

"I'm on my way."

I shut Colt's bedroom door and leaned against it. He had been crying nearly all night after I told him I had to cut his hair short, really short, to make it look okay.

I walked over to Alex's room and opened her door. She was already in bed and sound asleep. If I didn't know any better, I would say she had a smile on her face. I'd found out where she'd gotten the dye. It was from Luke, so Ari would be getting a phone call from me tomorrow.

I headed downstairs and smiled weakly at my mother. I made my way to the sofa and sat down next to her. "Mom, this is so much harder than I ever thought it would be."

She put her arm around me. "I know, baby, I know. You have to admit though, it was kind of funny."

I finally allowed myself to laugh. I nodded my head. "Yeah, it was."

We laughed a bit more, and then I was overcome with sadness. I glanced over to the clock on the mantel. It was now after ten.

"He'll be home soon, honey."

I took in a deep breath and let it out quickly. "Something is wrong, Mom. Gunner is never this late. He never misses a baseball game or soccer practice, and he is always home by the time the kids go to bed."

"Have you heard from him?"

I pulled out my cell phone and read his text message.

Gunner: Meeting ran late. Heading to dinner with client and Bill.

"Who's Bill?" my mother asked.

"The owner of the architecture firm. If he says jump, Gunner will jump."

My mother giggled. "Well, he won't be out too late. I heard his daddy saying they have to fix the pump outside the well house, so they're getting started early in the morning."

I nodded my head. "Yeah, Jeff called earlier to talk to Gunner about that."

My mother stood and stretched. "Are you okay now, darling? I should head back home before it gets too late. I'd better text Philip."

I got up and followed my mother to the kitchen. She grabbed her purse, pulled out her phone, and sent Philip, my stepfather, a text.

We walked out to her car, and I leaned in the window to kiss her cheek. "Thanks, Mom, for coming over and helping me. I'm not sure what's wrong with me. I just don't feel right."

She smiled and nodded her head. "Ellie, you're going through a hard time right now. I think you need to get out. Maybe you and Gunner should go away for a few days. You know Phil and I will watch the kids."

I smiled. "Mom, that would be so amazing. I'd love to get away for a couple of days."

"Plan a trip. We'll make it happen."

I kissed her one more time before saying good-bye. I watched the red taillights fade away as she drove down the driveway. I walked back into the house and picked up the home phone. I dialed Gunner's phone number. I pulled out my cell and looked at it to see if he sent a text.

"Hello?"

I was stunned at how loud the background noise was. "Gunner? Where are you? Are you still with the client and Bill?"

"Hey, sweetheart. Yeah, I am. I was just getting ready to leave. Bill, Karen, and I were about to walk out of the bar."

I didn't know what to be more shocked by—the fact that he was at a bar or that his client's name was Karen. I'd never even thought to ask for the name. It turned out the client I'd assumed was a *he* was really a *she*.

Karen?

"Did y'all eat at a bar?"

"What? I can't hear you. It's loud. Let me walk outside. Hold on."

I slowly started counting to ten.

One. Two. Three.

I'm so going to kill him.

Four. Five. Six.

Karen. Love how he failed to mention the client he's been meeting for lunches and dinners is a damn woman.

Seven. Eight. Nine.

"Ells, can you hear me now?"

"Yep. I asked, did you eat at the bar?"

He let out a chuckle. "Nah. Bill wanted to bring Karen to the brewery, so we walked over. I'm on my way."

"Well, I'm on my way to bed."

Silence.

"Ellie, are you upset?"

Stupid men. "Am I upset? Am I upset that you called me hours ago and said you would be late but not too late? Am I upset that you missed baseball and soccer practice—again? Am I upset that I had to shave our son's hair because *your* daughter decided to dye it with a color Luke had concocted, and then she cut chunks out of it? Am I upset that I had to sit with Colt while he cried for two hours before I put the kids to bed? Am I upset that I had to call my mother because I felt like I was having a nervous breakdown? And guess what? That's because my fucking husband is *never* home! *Ever!* He's out having lunch and dinner with *Karen.*"

"I'm going to go ahead and say you're upset."

I pulled the phone away and took a deep breath. "I'm going to bed. Be careful driving."

I hung up and slowly made my way to our bed. I stripped out of my clothes and put on one of Gunner's T-shirts. I crawled into bed and pulled my pillow next to my body.

Then, I cried until I fell asleep.

Chapter Two

Gunner

I PULLED UP behind Jeff's truck and put my truck in park. I dropped my head back against the seat and sat there for a minute.

Ellie had been asleep when I got home, and by the time I'd woken up, she had already been up and out of the house. When I'd walked into the kitchen, I'd seen Sharon sitting at the kitchen table, and I'd panicked. She'd informed me that Ellie had gone into Mason, and she would be home in a few hours.

I closed my eyes and tried to understand why Ellie was so angry.

The knock on the window caused me to quickly open my eyes. Jeff was standing there, staring at me.

I opened the truck door and smiled as I got out and made my way over to Jeff. "Shit, dude. Sorry you and Dad had to fix that pump without me. I got home late last night."

He nodded his head. "So I hear."

"What do you mean by that?"

He gave me a funny look and jerked his head slightly. "I mean just what I said. *So I hear.* Ari said Ellie is on a rampage because you've been staying out late, and she just found out the client you've been meeting with is a girl."

"So? What does that have to do with anything?"

Jeff placed the fence pullers on the bottom wire. He stopped and looked up at me. "Really, Mathews? Telling Ellie that your client is a female didn't seem important to you?"

I shook my head. "No, it didn't, and I still don't think it's important. I'm designing her home, and that's it. She's a very picky person, and I've had to meet her a few times to make changes. I've told Ellie this."

"Well, if you don't see anything wrong with it..."

I walked by him and grabbed the hooks for the fence. "I don't. I think Ellie is behaving like a spoiled brat."

He laughed. "Can I please be there when you tell her that? Please!"

I rolled my eyes and began working on the fence.

Jeff didn't say anything else to me until we were getting ready to head back to the house. He walked up to me, and I could see the concern on his face.

"Gunner, all I'm gonna say is that Ellie stays home with the kids day after day. She works her ass off, helping out with running this cattle ranch and with Ari's breeding business. When was the last time you took your wife out on a date?"

I shook my head as I felt the anger building inside me. "What are you saying, Jeff? I'm a shitty husband? When was the last time you took your wife out on a date?"

He gave me a shit-eating grin. "Don't push this back on me, dude. I'm actually taking Ari with me to Kentucky in a few weeks. It'll be just her and me for five days. I know we both need time to be alone together."

I let out a sigh and turned to get into my truck.

"Gunner, is everything okay with you and Ellie?"

I stopped dead in my tracks. I quickly spun around and stared at him. "Yes. Why would you even ask me that?"

He took a few steps back and gave me a look. "Because the guy who married my sister would never go to the bars and hang out with another woman while missing his kids' events, and I know for fucking sure, he would never call his wife a spoiled brat."

I stood there and took in Jeff's words. The more I thought about it, the more pissed off I got. "Ellie must be filling Ari in on everything." I wasn't sure why I'd said that. I was angry with myself more than anyone else.

For Jeff to think something was wrong between Ellie and me must mean that Ellie thought something was wrong.

"You know what? I'm walking away from this conversation, Gunner. For your sake, I really hope you don't ever do something you will regret. Ellie is my sister, but she is the best fucking thing to ever happen to you. If you hurt her in any way, dude, it's not going to be a happy ending for any of us."

He turned and walked to his truck. Before jumping in, he gave me one last look. Then, he peeled off and headed back to the main barn.

"Fuck." I got into my truck and headed in the same direction.

I watched as Jeff's truck turned and headed to the barn. I pulled up and parked outside of Gram and Gramp's house. I got out and made my way up the stairs.

Gramps stepped out the screen door and gave me one look. He shook his head. "Am I going to have to kick your ass?"

I smiled weakly. "No, sir."

"Let's go for a walk. I need some fresh air."

I followed him around the porch and down the steps. We started walking in silence.

Gramps cleared his throat. "What's going on, Drew? You look like you've got a heavy heart, son."

I pushed both my hands through my hair and let out a sigh. "Besides Jeff just basically accusing me of being a shitty husband and possibly cheating on my wife, I'm not really sure what's going on, Gramps."

He nodded his head. "Are you?"

My heart dropped, and I froze in my place. Gramps stopped walking and turned to look at me.

"How can you even ask me that?"

"Drew, I've had friends who loved their wives beyond belief, but they got tempted. They did things they later regretted, and most of them didn't even have an affair. The idea that they even thought about having an affair drove a wedge between them and their wives."

"I'm not having a fucking affair. I've just been busy with work. I've never thought about being with another woman— ever. It's just work."

"Work?"

I let out a deep breath. "Bill asked me to design a house. I said I'd love to. Gramps, I love designing, and honestly, I missed it."

"I thought you loved the ranch."

"I do love the ranch. I just needed a bit of a change. I needed something else to do, I guess."

Gramps nodded his head and began walking again. "I'm sure the way you were feeling is probably how Ellie feels as well, considering her day is filled with the same exact thing day after day."

Oh geesh. He's gonna lecture me about this, too.

10

Gramps stopped and turned to face me. "Drew, I'm only going to say this because, to be honest with you, I don't like the person you've become in the last month."

My mouth dropped open. "What?"

He shook his head. "What bothers me the most is that you don't even see it. You don't see how unhappy your wife has become. You don't see that when you miss your kids' practices or games, you're never going to be able to make that up. That moment in time is gone—forever."

I swallowed hard. "I'm not cheating on Ellie. It's never even crossed my mind, Gramps."

"Why did you come here today, Drew?"

I tilted my head. "What do you mean? I came here because I needed to talk to someone."

He gave me a weak smile. "The person you need to talk to isn't me, son. It's your wife."

My cell phone buzzed, scaring me. I never got a signal out here. I pulled it out and read the text message.

> Karen: Not happy at all with how the bathroom looks. I'm freaking out. When can you get here? I need this fixed, Drew. Now.

> Me: Can it wait until tomorrow? I need to spend some time with my wife.

> Karen: If you can't handle it, I'll call Bill. He'll take care of it.

"Fuck!" I dropped my head back and looked up at the sky. I was already tired from being out late with them last night and mending the fence all morning.

> Me: I'll be on my way in a few minutes. I've been working on the ranch all day, so I need to get cleaned up first.

> Karen: No. Now. I need this fixed. Now.

Me: Leaving now.

I looked at Gramps. "I have to go."

"To Ellie?"

I shook my head. "No, Karen isn't happy with something they are doing in the bathroom, and I need to see what's going on."

"The construction manager can't handle that? I mean, all you're responsible for was drawing up the plans."

I turned and began walking back to my truck. "No, Gramps, he can't because nine times out of ten, I'm drawing her a new plan."

I picked up my pace. I needed to get away from gramps, so I didn't have to listen to him telling me what a shit-ass husband and father I'd become. I walked up to my truck and opened the door.

I looked over the bed of the truck and smiled at my grandfather. "Thanks for the walk, Gramps."

He didn't smile back. He shook his head and walked away from me.

"Gramps, what am I supposed to do? I signed up for this job. I have to do it."

He turned and looked at me. "If it were me, I'd go home and tell my wife how much I love her. Maybe I'd even attempt to make love to her, and then I'd go and do the job if it were that important. It seems to me though that your wife should be more important."

I shook my head. "I can't do that, Gramps. I would if I could, but I can't. I'll talk to Ellie tonight."

I got in my truck and started it. I drove down the driveway, and I slammed my hand on the steering wheel. I stopped the truck and sent Ellie a text message.

Me: Hey, baby. I'm so sorry. I have to run to Fredericksburg. Karen, the client I've been working

with, isn't happy with her bathroom. I promise to make it up to you tonight. See if Mom and Dad can watch the kids. I'll take you to Austin for dinner. I love you.

Ellie replied before I took off driving again.

Ellie: Be careful. We'll see about tonight when you get home.

That's it? Shit. She is pissed.

Chapter Three

Ellie

I LOOKED IN the mirror at myself and smiled. I hadn't dressed up in forever. I glanced over at the clock. It was four thirty, and I'd heard nothing from Gunner. I sighed as I walked out of the bedroom. I went down the hall and into the living room.

I smiled when I saw Gunner's mom, Grace, sitting on the sofa with Alex on one side and Colt on the other.

Grace was reading to them, and when she glanced up, she did a double take. "Oh, Ellie. You look beautiful, darling."

Alex looked at me. "Mama, you look even more prettier than ever."

Colt jumped up and walked over to me. He stopped just in front of me and said, "I'm not sure Daddy is going to like you being all pretty, Mama."

I bent down and smiled as I tapped his nose. "Why do you say that, Colt?"

He scrunched up his nose. "'Cause all the boys will be looking at you. I've heard Daddy tell Uncle Jeff he doesn't like when other boys look at you. So, when you look so pretty, even more boys will be looking at you."

I felt the tears burning my eyes. I grabbed my son and pulled him to me as I attempted not to cry. "I love you, Colt Mathews. I love you so much."

When I pulled back, a tear ran down my cheek, and I quickly wiped it away. Colt smiled and then ran back over to Grace. She was smiling at me, but her face was filled with concern.

She handed the book to Alex and said, "Take over for a minute, honey. I have to talk to your mom."

Alex took the book and began reading to Colt. I loved seeing the two of them snuggled together on the sofa. They were not fighting for once.

Grace took my arm and led me into the kitchen. "What's wrong?"

I smiled. "Nothing. Colt just caught me off guard, that's all."

My cell phone went off, and I grabbed it from my purse.

Gunner: Baby, I'm so very sorry. I'm trying to get out of here. It's probably gonna be another hour at least.

I felt my heart drop, and my hands started shaking.

Me: Forget about going out. It will be too late.

Gunner: We can still go out to eat in town.

Me: Where, Gunner? The local diner? No, thanks. Don't worry about it. Take care of Karen and her needs. Clearly, she is more important.

Gunner: Ellie, don't do this. Please. I'm really sorry.

Me: So am I, Gunner. More than you know.

Gunner: What does that mean?

Me: Go to dinner with Karen because I'm done.

I turned off my phone and looked at Grace. I didn't even care that tears were now spilling from my eyes. "He's not going to be home for at least another hour. Do you mind watching the kids until I can call my mother?"

Grace looked confused. "Why do you need to call your mother?"

I swallowed hard. "I have to get away, Grace. I feel like I'm losing my damn mind. I need a few days to clear my head."

Grace began shaking her head. "Ellie, no. Don't do this."

I looked her in the eyes. "I remember a story you told me once. You left Jack. Do you remember telling me that story, Grace?"

She slowly nodded. "I do."

"I'm not leaving my husband or my children, Grace. I just need to get out of here. I need time to think."

"Don't worry about calling your mother. Jack and I will stay with the kids, and I'll call her in the morning to let her know what's going on. I'm pretty sure she is working at the hospital tonight anyway."

Shit. I forgot she picked up a shift tonight.

I smiled weakly. "I need this, Grace. I just need some time to understand things, like why I feel the way I do."

"Honey, I think what you need is to talk to Gunner. You both need to talk this through."

"I've tried, Grace. Something about him is off. He doesn't want to listen. He just keeps blowing off my concerns."

"Ellie, he loves you so much. You have to know that he would never do anything to hurt you."

I nodded my head and wiped away my tears. "I'm going to change and head out."

I walked past her and glanced at Alex and Colt. I began crying harder, so I picked up my pace and practically ran to my bedroom.

I packed a small overnight bag. I just needed one night to clear my head and be alone with my thoughts.

Just one night.

I shut the door to the hotel room and leaned against it. I smiled as I looked at the same room Gunner and I had stayed in before. I closed my eyes, and I could almost feel his lips on my skin. Then, I started crying again.

What in the hell is wrong with me?

I exhaled a deep breath and made my way over to the bed. I sat down and looked around. "Why did I decide to stay here?"

I reached for the phone and dialed Ari's phone number.

"Hello?"

"Ari, it's me."

"Oh, yes. Hold on just one minute, please."

I heard Ari telling Jeff that she was stepping outside to take a call.

"Jesus H. Christ, Ellie. Where are you?"

My mouth dropped open, and I went to talk, but Ari cut me off.

"Gunner has flipped out. I mean, he has flipped out."

"What? How do you know?"

"I know because his ass is standing in my kitchen. He's been begging Jeff and me to tell him where you are."

I looked at the clock. I'd only been gone for around two hours. "What did Grace tell him?"

Ari let out a sigh. "She told him that you said you needed some time to clear your head and think. I'm telling you, Ellie, I've never in my life seen Gunner so freaked out. If I wasn't worried he might have heart failure, I'd use this opportunity to screw with him."

"Good. He should be freaked out. He hasn't seemed to care where or what I've been doing for the last few weeks."

"Ellie, I don't want to be dragged into this, and I'm not saying who is right. All I am saying is, don't you think you should have maybe stayed and talked to him? Maybe he doesn't realize how badly he has been ignoring you and the kids."

I swallowed hard. "He knows, Ari. I've tried talking to him, and he blew me off. He just said he wanted this one opportunity to design something big. The fact that he withheld his late-night meetings were with a female client doesn't sit well with me. Why did he feel the need to keep that a secret? If he had told me, I'd be okay. All I'm doing now is wondering why he hid it. If he hid that, what else is he hiding?"

Ari covered the phone and said something to someone else. "Ellie, I think Jeff knows I'm talking to you. What do I do? What do I say?"

"I'm sorry I put y'all in the middle of it."

"Ellie, do you honestly think Gunner would ever cheat on you?"

I looked down at the floor and closed my eyes. "If you asked me that same question two weeks ago, I would have said never. Last night, when he came home from a meeting with Karen and Bill, he was standing on the porch, talking to her on the phone. I was on the other side of the door. I was going to open it, but then he started talking to her. Why was he talking to her that late at night when they just left each other?"

"What was he saying?"

"He told her that he understood why she was being picky and that he would do whatever it takes to make her happy with the design."

"Ellie, you are reading way too much into this."

Then, I heard Gunner's voice. *Shit.*

"Ah hell, get ready to grab the phone," Ari said.

"Ellie? My God, what are you doing? Where are you?"

The sound of Gunner's panicked voice caused my heart to drop, but a part of me was glad he was worried. It served him right.

"I, um...I'm fine, Gunner. May I please speak with Ari?"

"Baby, please come back home. I swear to you, Ellie, I would never do anything to hurt you or the kids. Y'all are my life. Please...just stop acting like this, and come home."

And there it was. He was being the Gunner from the last two weeks, the one who had kept accusing me of acting like a child.

I stood up and balled my hand into a fist. "That is exactly why I left. Please enlighten me, Gunner, as to how I'm acting. Like a spoiled brat? A child maybe? Jealous and bored housewife perhaps?"

He sighed. "Ellie, I don't think you're any of that. I've just been really stressed out with this job, and I want to do a good job for Bill."

"Why, Gunner? You have a job. You own one of the biggest cattle companies in central Texas. You're a partner in a fast-growing breeding business. You're a father to two beautiful kids who hardly got to see their father before he took on his new job. And as far as I'm concerned, when was the last time you touched me or held me in your arms or told me you loved me?"

"Ells..."

"I can tell you when the last time was—the night you went to your first evening meeting with your *client*."

"I swear to you, nothing has happened. I have no feelings for her. What do I have to do to prove that to you?"

A sob escaped my mouth. "I think we need to be apart for a few days. My mother can help with the kids. I'll call her, and—"

I heard Gunner crying, and my whole world shattered.

"Ellie, no. Please don't leave me."

I took in a deep breath. "I'm not leaving you. I love you, Gunner, more than the air I breathe. I feel like I've been slowly losing myself the last few months, and then after all this with your new job, I just need some time to myself. I'll call the kids in the morning."

"Ellie, wait. Just tell me where you are."

"I love you, Drew."

I quickly hung up the phone. I lay down on the bed and slowly let myself fall apart.

What did I just do?

Oh God, what did I just do?

Chapter Four

Gunner

"**DADDY, IS MOMMY** going to be calling soon? She was gonna call after dinner."

I glanced up and smiled at Colt. Alex and Colt were sitting on the kitchen island, watching me make their lunches for tomorrow.

"Yeah, buddy. She'll call soon."

Alex looked at me, and I swore, she had tears in her eyes. I tried to smile bigger, but she looked away from me.

"Daddy, is Mama coming back home? She started crying this morning on the phone. She sounded so sad when I talked to her."

My heart felt as if it had just been ripped open. "Baby girl, come here."

I bent down as Alex jumped off her seat at the island. She walked into my arms, and I held her as tightly as I could.

"Of course, she's coming home. She is sad, honey. She hates being away from you and Colt."

Alex pulled back, and her blue eyes caught mine. "Then, why did she leave? When she left, she told me she was only going to be gone for one night. It's been three already. To-night will make four. I want her to come home."

I closed my eyes and then opened them. "I'm so sorry, Alex. Daddy wasn't being a very good daddy or husband to y'all. Mommy just needed to...she needed to..."

The phone started ringing, and I silently thanked God that Ellie was calling early.

Alex pushed out of my arms and ran for the phone. "Mama! Colt, it's Mama!"

I helped Colt down from his seat and watched him run over to Alex. I stood there and listened to them each take turns talking to Ellie. Each night, she had hung up before I could even talk to her. If she were trying to teach me a les-son, she had succeeded.

Colt looked at me and smiled. "Oh no, Mama. Grams hasn't been over in two days. Yes, ma'am. Daddy has been. He's been making us breakfast each morning, and he's even packed our lunches."

Colt turned away from me a little and attempted to whisper, "He really doesn't know what to pack us. He put a cheese stick in my lunch."

I let out a chuckle.

Alex laughed. "Let me talk to her again, Colt."

"I love you, Mama. Please come home soon. We all miss you. Yes, ma'am, I will. Night. I love you," Colt said before handing the phone to Alex.

"Mama, yes. Yes, ma'am." Alex looked at me. "Yes. No, Daddy picks us up from the bus stop."

I smiled slightly. I knew Ellie was asking Alex a million questions about who was taking care of things.

I turned around, opened the dishwasher, and began loading our dinner plates. The last few days had really shown me how much Ellie did around the house. I wanted to kick my own ass for taking her for granted.

"He, um...well, he turned my white shirt to pink by mistake."

I smiled. Neither of my children were good at whispering.

"Um...sad. Yeah, I mean, he looks *really* sad."

I turned and looked at Alex. She smiled and gave me a thumbs-up. My mouth dropped open.

"Okay, Mama. I love you, too." She hung up the phone and looked at Colt. "Mama said to make sure you get your reading in."

"Ah, man!" Colt said as he stomped out of the kitchen.

Alex walked up to stand beside me, and she smiled. "Mama said she misses you."

I nodded my head and smiled slightly.

"Daddy, why are y'all not talking to each other?"

I sucked in a breath and slowly blew it out. "I wish I knew, kiddo. Grown-up stuff, I guess."

She nodded her head. "Do you know where she is, Dad?"

The way Alex had just called me *Dad* made me stop and look at her. My baby girl was growing up.

I placed my hand on the side of her face. "You look so much like your mother. You're both so beautiful."

She blushed and looked away before looking back at me. She shrugged her shoulders. "I overheard Aunt Ari telling Grace that Mommy needed some time to think. I don't know what she is thinking about, but I bet she's thinking of you, Daddy. She asked me a lot of questions about you. She even asked how you looked, and I told her sad. She said she thought she probably looked sad, too, but she was in a place that had happy memories of the two of you."

In that moment, I had an idea of where Ellie might be.

I bent down and looked into Alex's eyes. "Alex, did she tell you anything else about where she is?"

She smiled. "No, but she did say she had walked on a trail around a lake. I'm not sure which lake she was talking about. But, Daddy, she said she is coming home tomorrow. I don't think she told Colt that. I bet she wants to surprise him."

I grinned and said, "I bet. Alex, I need to make a phone call, sweetheart. Go get your homework done before bedtime."

She nodded and walked out of the kitchen. I walked over to the phone and dialed my parents' number.

"Hello?"

"Mom! I need a huge favor."

My mother laughed. "You think you know where she is?"

"I do. Can you take care of the kids tonight and get them to school tomorrow?"

"Of course." She pulled the phone away and said, "Jack, we're gonna spend the night at Drew's."

I quickly put the kids' lunches in the refrigerator and made my way to our bedroom.

"We'll be there in a few minutes."

"Thanks, Mom. I owe you and Dad big time."

She chuckled. "Just go get her and bring her home already."

"Oh, I intend to, Mom. I intend to."

I stepped out of the elevator and made my way down the hallway of The Driskill hotel. I smiled as I stopped and stood in front of the room where Ellie and I had spent our honeymoon. I pushed my hand through my hair and counted down from ten. My hands were shaking, and for some reason, I was scared to death she would open the door and shut it in my face.

I knocked and held my breath.

When the door opened and she saw me, her eyes lit up, and the biggest smile spread across her face. "Drew."

I smiled and slowly let out the breath I had been holding. "Ellie."

She shook her head. "How did you know where to find me? I told Alex I would be home tomorrow. What are you doing here?"

I started walking into the room as she began walking backward.

"I'm here to make love to my wife."

Ellie's eyes changed and held that familiar passion I loved so much. I shut the door behind me.

She bit down on her lower lip and whispered, "I was hoping you would figure out where I was."

I walked up to her and placed my hands on the sides of her face. I leaned down and kissed her. She placed her hands on my chest and moaned as our tongues began dancing together.

The kiss was slow and sweet at first. I just wanted to take it slow. I'd missed her so much the last few days. I wanted to take every single thing in—the feel of her lips on mine, the smell of her hair, and the warmth of her touch.

I pulled my lips from hers and watched as a tear made its way down her beautiful face. I gently wiped it away.

She said, "Gunner, I've missed you so much."

"I promise you, Ellie, I will never make you feel lost again. Knowing I made you doubt our love kills me. I intend on making it up to you...all night."

She smiled. "That sounds like a good plan."

I took a step back and slowly lifted my T-shirt up and over my head. I unbuttoned my pants and pushed them down, allowing my dick to spring free. I watched her eyes travel up and down my body as she took me in. When she licked her lips, I wanted to bury myself so deep inside her that she would never again doubt my love for her.

"Undress yourself, Ells."

I almost laughed when I watched her pull her shirt over her head. She quickly pushed her shorts and panties down before kicking them off to the side of the room.

"Gunner, I need to feel you."

I walked up to her and grabbed her. I pulled her to me and lifted her up. She wrapped her legs around me, and my knees felt weak just from having her in my arms.

I loved her so much.

I walked over to the bed and gently laid her on it as I smiled down at her. "I'm going to make love to you now, baby."

"Yes," she whispered.

She opened herself to me and arched her back. I crawled over her and placed my hands on the sides of her face as I teased her entrance with my dick.

"Do not ever doubt my love," I said as I slowly began pushing into her.

Her eyes lit up with passion, and I slammed my lips to hers. When she pushed her hands through my hair, I let out a moan and began moving faster. She tightened her legs around me, and I lost control. I had wanted to slowly make love to her, but something had happened and I needed to take her fast and hard. We were both aching to get more.

I moved up and grabbed her hips as I slammed in and out of her.

"Yes. Gunner...harder. Faster, please go deeper."

I gave her just what she needed. I could almost feel her squeezing around my dick.

"Oh God. I'm coming. Oh...Gunner..."

She grabbed the sheets and began calling out my name as I pushed deep inside of her. I tried to hold off but couldn't. I called out her name as an intense orgasm hit me fast and hard. I moved in and out until every last drop was out, and then I collapsed next to her on the bed. We were both breathing as if we had just run a marathon.

Ellie rolled over, threw her leg over me, and nestled her head into my neck. "I've missed you. I've missed this," she whispered.

I pulled her closer to me and kissed her forehead. "I've missed it, too, baby. I'm so sorry, Ellie. I never meant to make you feel like you weren't wanted. I'll never forgive myself for hurting you."

She moved back some and tilted her head, looking at me. "Gunner, I just don't want to fall into a routine where every day is the same thing. I want you to sneak me off to the barn like we did before. I want to make out in the back of a movie theater or have sex in your truck. I just want...us."

I moved her body up some and began kissing her. She always tasted so sweet. I rolled her over and laid her down on the bed as I moved my hand between her legs. She instantly opened to me, and I pushed my fingers inside her. I began massaging the spot that I knew drove her over the edge. She grabbed a handful of my hair and smiled.

"I'm going to make you come again, baby."

She closed her eyes and started moving her hips. "Gunner...oh God...don't stop. I'm...so...close."

I leaned down and began sucking on her nipple, and she jerked as her orgasm hit her. I bit down on her nipple.

She cried out, "Yes! Gunner, yes! Oh God. Oh...God... yes!"

I loved making Ellie come. She was so responsive to my touch, even after all these years.

She opened her eyes as she smiled at me, and I kissed her nose.

Getting off the bed, I stood up and reached for her hand. "Come on, let's go take a shower."

She nodded her head and stood up. I leaned down, picked her up, and began carrying her into the bathroom. I set her down on the bench, turned around, and started the shower.

Ellie cleared her throat. "Can I ask you something?"

I glanced back at her as I checked the water temperature. "Of course you can."

She looked down and then back up at me. "How were you taking care of the kids by yourself with having to work on the ranch and...work with Karen?"

The mention of Karen's name made my skin crawl. The day after Ellie had left, I'd called Karen to meet me for lunch. I'd let her know that I was stepping down from my position as her architect and that Bill would be able to finish up. She had seemed okay with it. She'd even acted sympathetic. I had excused myself to head to the restroom. She'd walked into the restroom and locked the door behind her before she began undressing. I'd about had heart failure. When I'd asked her to stop, she'd gotten angry and said she knew I wanted to fuck her. I'd quickly pushed her out of the way and unlocked the door. Heading to my truck, I'd called Bill and told him I was done.

"I told Bill I was done and that the job was taking time away from my family and causing issues between us. I love you too much, Ellie, to ever let something like this happen again."

I held out my hand and led her into the shower. I began soaping her body. "Ells, you have to promise me that you'll talk to me if you ever feel like this again. Please don't ever leave me again. You have no idea how devastated I was."

Her eyes searched my face, and when I saw the tears beginning to fall, I leaned down and kissed her. I pushed her against the wall, and I began moaning when she started playing with my dick. I pulled my lips from hers when I felt myself hardening in her hand.

"Drew, make love to me."

I reached over and turned off the shower. I grabbed a towel, and I started to dry off Ellie and then myself. I picked her up and carried her back to the bed.

"Lie back, baby."

I crawled over her and grabbed her hands, placing them over her head. I used my right hand to wipe away another tear. I pushed gently into my beautiful wife and began making love to her. Our bodies felt as one as I moved slowly inside her.

When I felt myself getting closer to coming, I leaned down and brushed my lips against hers. "I'm about to come, baby," I whispered.

She closed her eyes and arched her body, and we both began whispering each other's names.

In that moment, I vowed I would never again take my wife for granted. She, and only she, could make me feel so loved and so wanted.

Chapter Five

Ellie

I PEEKED MY eyes open and saw the daylight shining through the side of the curtain. I turned my head slightly and smiled when I saw Gunner sleeping peacefully. I tried to remember the last time either one of us had gotten to sleep in.

I moved just a bit, and I felt the soreness in my body. Gunner and I had made love four times. The first was raw and fast, and I loved it. Then, we'd done it again after the shower. The third time, Gunner had woken me up at one in the morning and made love to me again. When I'd crawled on top of him at five thirty this morning, I had needed something different. I'd needed to be fucked hard and fast, and Gunner had done just that. I was pretty sure I would have small bruises on my hips from where he had gripped me.

I stretched and smiled. I rolled over and grabbed my cell phone. Grace had texted and said Alex and Colt had gone off to school this morning. Then, I read my mother's text.

> **Mom:** I've arranged for the next two days off. I talked to Jeff and Josh, and they will take care of

everything on the ranch. You and Gunner stay in
Austin for another couple of days and relax with
each other. I love you, Ellie.

I felt my stomach jump a bit, and I was sure I was grinning from ear to ear. I couldn't wait to tell Gunner that we had two more days to be with each other.

Me: Mom, you don't know how much this means to
me. Thank you!

Mom: Trust me, I know. Get lost in each other again,
baby girl.

I blushed at my mother's text and then hit Reply.

Me: Yes, ma'am. I intend on doing a lot more than
that!

I giggled, and then I felt Gunner wrap his arms around me.

"Mmm...you smell like heaven," he whispered against my neck.

"You smell pretty yummy yourself."

He began moving his fingers up and down my arm, leaving a burning sensation in their path. I was shocked by how he could still give me goose bumps after all these years.

"I don't want to go back yet," he whispered.

I rolled over and smiled as I pushed my hand through his hair and stared into his beautiful blue eyes. "We don't have to."

He tilted his head and gave me a questioning look. "We don't?" He chuckled. "I'm pretty sure our children would miss us if we didn't head back."

I laughed. "I mean, we still have two days. My mom texted me and said she made arrangements with Jeff and Josh, so we can stay for another two days."

The smile that spread across his face caused me to grin.

"I know what I want to do then," he said.

"Oh, yeah? What?"

He shook his head. "It's a surprise. Let's get up and get dressed. Wear jeans. Did you bring a jacket? I think it's going to be cool today."

I got up and laughed. "Yes, Dad. I brought a sweatshirt. That should be good."

Gunner jumped up and walked into the bathroom. I watched as he walked by naked. We hardly ever walked around naked anymore, not with the chance of a little one running in on us.

I bit down on my lip. I couldn't believe I wanted him again. I was about to walk into the bathroom and make my move when someone knocked on the door.

"Room service, Mr. and Mrs. Mathews."

Gunner poked his head out of the bathroom. "Did you order room service?"

Shaking my head, I grabbed my robe and put it on. I slowly opened the door and smiled. "Um...we didn't order room service," I said.

The young man's face blushed, and he looked away quickly. "It's from Ari, ma'am," he said.

I tilted my head and looked at him. "Ari?"

"Yes, um...so, yeah...okay...well, enjoy your stay, Mrs. Mathews." He quickly turned and began walking away.

"Oh, wait...a tip," I called out.

He turned and smiled big. "Mrs. Johnson paid me handsomely. No tip needed."

I shook my head and pulled the cart into the room.

Gunner came up behind me and wrapped his arms around me. "What's Ari up to? Jesus, did she order enough food for an army or what?"

I shrugged my shoulders and lifted the two metal pans at the same time. I let out a gasp as Gunner began laughing his ass off.

"Damn, that girl was always my favorite of your friends," Gunner said as he picked up the handcuffs and winked at me.

I looked back down and saw a brand-new vibrator, a Victoria's Secret bag, and massage oil.

My mouth dropped open, and I turned to Gunner. "Oh. My. God. Do you think she paid that poor boy to go out and buy this stuff?"

Gunner really lost it, and he started laughing even harder. He pulled me to him as I began giggling.

"I can't wait to get you back here this afternoon and have my wicked way with you."

I felt the heat move between my legs as my stomach clenched. I wanted him to have his wicked way with me right now. I looked up and tilted my head down and batted my eyelashes.

"Oh no, get dressed, sweetheart. I have a full day planned for us."

Gunner pulled into the parking lot of the Magnolia Café. I smiled as all the memories came flooding back to me. Gunner, Jeff, Ari, and I used to come here all the time for breakfast. It seems like it was just yesterday.

I slid into a booth, and Gunner slid in next to me. His arm brushed against my body, and I couldn't believe the butterflies that took off in my stomach. I smiled as I looked down at the goose bumps covering my arms. I loved that his touch still affected me the way it did.

Gunner looked at me and asked, "Tea?"

I nodded my head and sat back, letting my husband take control.

"We'll both have a cup of hot tea, two of the house special omelets, and a cup of fresh fruit, please."

I watched as the waitress practically eye-fucked my husband while he gave our order. Gunner didn't look like he was in his mid-thirties at all. He still ran every day, and his body was beyond amazing. His perfectly tanned skin was always so soft. I smiled as I thought back to when Gunner had first taken over the ranch, and Garrett had told him that sunscreen was the next best thing to a woman. I glanced up at the waitress who seemed to have just noticed me sitting there.

She smiled and looked back at Gunner. "I'll have those teas as well as two glasses of water right out."

"Thank you," Gunner said.

He placed his hand on my knee, causing me to jump a little from just his touch.

He looked at me after the waitress walked off and smiled that damn crooked smile of his. "Did I scare you, baby?"

I shook my head. "No, your touch seems to be driving me slightly crazy today."

His eyes lit up, and he leaned closer to me as he whispered into my ear, "Too bad I had you put jeans on. I bet I could have driven you even crazier by giving you an orgasm right here in the booth."

I swallowed hard at the idea of Gunner touching me in public. I slowly grinned and said, "We still have another day, if you think you can really go through with something like that."

Gunner sucked in a breath of air and then looked down at my lips. "Is that a challenge, Mrs. Mathews?"

I let out a giggle. "Yes, I believe it is, Mr. Mathews."

"Let's just say that I'm...up for the challenge."

When the waitress cleared her throat, Gunner squeezed my leg, and my whole body came to attention.

Public orgasm...a vibrator and handcuffs....Gunner all to myself.

Oh, yeah, this is going to be the best couple of days of my life.

Chapter Six

Gunner

THE WHOLE TIME we were eating breakfast, I couldn't stop thinking about what Ellie had said. My dick was so fucking hard that I could hardly stand it. She kept looking at me as she ate her omelet, and I knew what was running through her mind.

I needed to make sure I planned things like this for us more often. Maybe I could take her somewhere once a month. Even to a bed-and-breakfast in Fredericksburg would be a nice getaway.

We finished eating, and I paid our bill. I grabbed Ellie's hand and led her out to my truck. I opened the door and helped her in. As she sat down, I slipped my hand up her shirt and quickly under her bra. I pinched her nipple, and she let out a gasp before biting down on her lip.

"I want you, Ellie," I whispered.

Her beautiful blue eyes met mine as she smiled. "I want you, too."

I pulled my hand out and watched as she adjusted her bra. I shut the door, and I adjusted myself as I made my way to the driver's side. I got in the truck and began to drive out of the parking lot. Ellie took my hand in hers and began moving her thumb across my skin. Just the soft, slow movement was driving me to the edge.

I started heading toward Zilker Park.

Ellie asked, "Where to now, captain?"

"It's a surprise," I said as I glanced over at her.

She smiled at me, and I about melted. I loved her so much. Her smile would forever be my undoing.

"Hmm...well, you're not heading back to the hotel, and honestly, the only thing I want right now is your dick buried deep inside me."

I about slammed on the brakes as my heart took a deep dive to my stomach. I looked at Ellie as she continued to look straight ahead as if she hadn't even said a single word.

Fuck the canoe ride. I need my wife.

I put my signal on and turned down a side road. I didn't even care that I was pulling into a neighborhood. I parked on the side of the road. "Get in the backseat, Ellie."

I saw her peek at me before she unbuckled her seat belt and climbed into the back. I quickly got out of the truck and made my way to the backseat. I opened the door and had to hang on for dear life. My wife was sitting there in a white lace bra and matching thong panties.

"Ellie...you're so beautiful."

"I'm waiting."

I jumped in and shut the door. Ellie frantically pulled my boots off as I lifted my T-shirt over my head.

"Shit, Ellie. I'm so damn turned-on right now. I might not last long."

She smiled as she unbuttoned my jeans. I leaned back and pulled them off my body, letting my dick spring to attention. She moved back away from me and leaned against the back passenger door. The moment she pushed her hand into her panties, I knew what she wanted. I quickly moved to her and pulled her hand out. I pulled her panties out of the way and began tasting my sweet wife. She grabbed a fistful of my hair and made the sweetest moans I'd ever heard. I buried my face between her legs, sucking and licking, until she started calling out my name.

"Gunner, I'm going to come. Oh God, yes!"

When she finally came down from her orgasm, I got up and began taking her panties off. I slid her down until she was lying on the bench seat.

"I'm gonna fuck you now, Ellie."

She smiled and closed her eyes before opening them and looking into my eyes. "Yes, Gunner...yes."

I slammed my dick so fast and hard into her that she let out a whimper.

When I pulled out, she said in a panicked voice, "No, harder. Please, Gunner, I need to feel you. I need it hard and fast."

I about died. There was nothing sexier than my sweet wife talking dirty to me. I pushed into her again as deep as I could go.

"Oh God, yes."

I pulled out and grabbed her hips, and then I gave her just what she'd asked for.

"Yes. Yes. Gunner, I'm going to come again. Harder!" Ellie cried out.

I was doing everything possible to hold off. Watching Ellie's reactions was almost more than I could handle. Something was happening between us. We were rekindling what we'd almost lost. We were getting it back, and I'd never felt so alive in my life.

When Ellie began calling out my name, I pulled out and pushed into her again, deeper and harder. I could feel her squeezing down on my dick, and that was my undoing.

"God, Ellie, I'm coming, baby. Ah, baby, it feels so good."

I was panting hard as Ellie wrapped her whole body around mine. I slid down next to her in the truck and pulled her as close to me as I could.

"I've missed you," she whispered.

I closed my eyes and fought like hell to hold back my tears. "I'll never let you miss me again, Ells. Never."

Ellie and I just talked as we lay entangled in the back-seat for the longest time. We talked about everything—our feelings for each other, the kids, our future, and the ranch. It was almost as if we were catching up on months of not seeing each other.

"Ellie, I want to do something like this once a month. I think we need to start taking just a few days for you and me."

"I would love that, Gunner, even if we just stayed in a hotel for a day or two. I just want this, the way we used to be, without trying to be quiet so that the kids don't hear. I want to just let loose once in a while."

"Then, it's a plan. I'll make the arrangements for next month."

She sat up and looked at me. "I'm so sorry I was a jealous idiot. I didn't mean for you to quit the job."

I smiled and said, "I'm glad you did. I needed the eye-opener." I sat up and began handing back her clothes. "Come on. We still have a few more things to do before I take you back to the hotel, so we can really have some fun."

When I pulled into Zilker Park, Ellie started laughing. "Oh my gosh. Are we going for a canoe ride?"

I nodded my head and smiled. "Yep." I parked, jumped out of the truck, and jogged around to her side. I opened the door and held out my hand. "Don't forget your sweatshirt."

She grabbed it and jumped out of the truck. As we walked down to the water, I had a flashback to the day I'd brought her here. That day, I'd known I was in love with her and that I would love her always.

The song "Let Me Love You" by Neyo popped into my head, and my stomach did a crazy flip. I stopped walking, and Ellie turned to look at me. I just stood there and stared at her.

She slowly smiled and tilted her head. "What's wrong?"

"I was just thinking about the first time we were here. Do you remember that day, Ellie?"

She nodded her head. "I do. We kissed for the first time down on the hike-and-bike trail."

I chuckled. "Yeah, we did."

I grabbed her other hand and pulled her closer to me. "I'll always love you. Please don't ever forget that, Ellie. You're my everything. You're my entire world. If I didn't have you..." I shook my head and looked into her eyes. "I don't even want to think about it. I promise to make you smile every single day, and I'll never again bring a sad or hurtful tear to your eyes. I promise you."

A tear rolled down her face. "I love you, Drew."

"I love you more, Ellie."

Chapter Seven

Ellie

I SAT BACK and felt the sun warming my face. It was slightly chilly out today, especially with us being on the water.

"Are you enjoying yourself, sweetheart?" Gunner asked.

I lifted my head and looked at him. I couldn't help but smile. He was so breathtakingly handsome. His brown hair was slightly wavy, and his smile—*oh Lord, how that smile makes me do things I never thought I'd do.*

"I am—more than you could ever imagine. It's amazing to just sit here and relax. There are no fighting kids, no weeds to pull in the garden, no soccer practice, no PTA meetings..."

I let out a sigh, and Gunner chuckled.

"You love all that other stuff though. Don't you?"

I nodded my head. "Yeah, I do. But I think everyone needs a little bit of *me* time...or *we* time. I needed *we* time."

"I agree. I needed some *we* time, too." He took off his sunglasses and looked at me.

By the look in his eyes, I could tell he was up to something. He began rowing over to the side of the river.

I looked around and said, "What are you doing?"

The left corner of his mouth rose slightly, and he laughed. "Baby, you challenged me. It's time to show you I was serious."

I sat up straight. "Huh? We already had sex in the truck."

He threw his head back and laughed. "Nah, that wasn't public enough."

My heart began to pound as I tried to figure out what Gunner was up to. He pulled up to the bank of the river and carefully got out of the canoe.

He reached his hand out for me. "Be careful, baby. Come on."

I stood up and took his hand as he helped me out. He lifted the canoe out of the water and pulled it up onto the dirt path. A few feet above us was the hike-and-bike trail. I could hear people running by. I took a step over, looked up, and saw an older lady riding her bike.

I snapped my head back and looked at him. "No way, Gunner."

He slowly nodded his head. "Oh, yes, ma'am. You can't challenge me and then back out of it. I intend on making you orgasm right up against that tree."

He pointed, and I turned around to see a giant cypress tree. I swallowed hard and felt my stomach clench. The idea of it thrilled me. I decided two could play at this game. I spun back around and looked out at the lake. Hardly anyone was on the lake since it was a weekday and chilly. I kicked off my sneakers and began unbuttoning my pants. Gunner licked his lips as I slid my pants down. Goose bumps covered my body, but it wasn't because it was cold out. It was from the way Gunner was looking at me with hungry eyes.

I took my jeans and put them over a nearby branch as I watched Gunner unbutton his jeans.

"Holy hell, baby. You're driving me crazy."

He reached in and adjusted himself as I smiled.

I used my finger and motioned for him to come toward me. "I'm not walking over there without shoes on."

Gunner smiled bigger and picked me up so quickly that I let out a small cry. I looked up and could barely see someone running by through the trees. Gunner walked us over to the cypress tree. I'd expected him to just pleasure me with his fingers, but when he leaned me against the tree, he pushed my panties out of the way and began teasing me with his tip. I was so overcome with what we were doing that I almost came on the spot.

"Oh God, Gunner. I'm going to come fast. It's already building up," I whispered.

He smiled. "Hold on, baby, you're about to take the ride of your life."

Before I could even say anything, he pushed inside me and began moving. Somehow, Gunner always knew the spot to hit to make me come fast and hard. He leaned down and began kissing my neck. The sounds of dogs barking and people talking, running, or riding their bikes were beginning to blend with my low moans of pleasure. I quickly looked out toward the water, and we were barely covered by all the tree branches. If someone looked hard enough, they would see what we were doing.

A warm feeling ran through my body, and I felt my orgasm building. Then, I heard a woman talking.

"So, Laura said the report is due back by five. That's why she couldn't join us."

Two women had stopped practically right above us.

I closed my eyes as Gunner slowed down, and then he pushed inside me harder.

"Come, baby," he whispered. He gently bit on my ear-lobe.

I placed my hands on his shoulders and began moving right along with him. I needed to feel more of him.

"Deeper," I whispered.

"Well, that's a shame. Laura was so looking forward to coming today."

I closed my eyes and whispered, "So am I."

Gunner pulled back, and I opened my eyes. He slowly smiled, and I let out a giggle. He pressed his lips to mine. The kiss started slow and sweet but quickly turned passionate. I pulled back and dropped my head against the tree. I began moving hips to meet Gunner's movements.

Oh God. He's so deep. It feels so good.

"Faster, Gunner, go faster." I didn't even care that I hadn't whispered.

The two women had either moved on or stopped talking. All I heard was Gunner's body hitting mine as he moved in and out, harder and faster.

It took everything out of me not to let out a scream when my orgasm hit me. I whimpered, and Gunner captured my lips with his. He kissed me, and my orgasm seemed to go on forever.

He poured himself into me as he whispered, "Fuck. Fucking hell, Ellie, it feels so good."

Gunner and I rested our foreheads against each other as we tried to catch our breaths.

"I'm getting too old for this shit," Gunner said as he looked at me and smiled.

I let out a laugh and hit him on the shoulder. Gunner looked up, and I did the same.

"Do you think they heard us?" I asked in a whisper.

I peeked back at Gunner, and he was smiling so big that it caused me to giggle.

"I'm pretty damn sure they heard us."

I bit my lower lip. "You certainly rose to the challenge, Mr. Mathews."

He laughed and began carrying me back toward my jeans and sneakers. He set me down gently and stood in front of me while I quickly got dressed.

I slipped on my sneakers. "God, I can't wait to tell Ari this."

Gunner shook his head and pushed the canoe back into the water. "Come on, I have another place I want to go."

"More public sex?"

He helped me into the canoe and shook his head. "No, ma'am. No more of that. I was scared shitless someone would see you."

I sat down in the canoe and watched as he got in and pushed away from the shoreline. My whole body was still on fire, and I couldn't help but feel happy, knowing Gunner had worried that someone might me.

He looked at me and said, "What was that like for you, Ells?"

I felt my face instantly redden. "I thought it was hot. I don't think I've had an orgasm like that in a while."

He chortled. "Hot doesn't even begin to describe that, baby. It was beyond hot."

I nodded my head. "Yeah, it was. It's not something you'd think a couple with two kids would be doing after being married for so long."

"I feel another challenge coming on."

I laughed. "No! No more challenges."

Chapter Eight

Gunner

THE SECOND I turned down Fourth Street, Ellie started clapping her hands. "Oh my God! We're going to Halcyon, aren't we?"

I chuckled. "Yep."

"Oh, Gunner, I can't even believe how incredibly romantic you are."

I pulled into the valet parking, and a young kid walked up with a cocky little grin on his face.

"Wow, dude, nice truck."

I smiled. "Yeah, it is. You put a scratch on it, and I'll hang you up by your balls."

"Gunner!" Ellie walked over to me and hit me in the stomach.

The kid's smile faded, and he nodded his head. "Yes, sir. Not a scratch, sir."

I put my arm around Ellie's waist and began walking her to the Halcyon.

When we walked in, I was flooded by memories. This day was exactly what we'd needed.

"Oh, Gunner, today was exactly what we needed."

I stopped and looked at her. "Ellie, I was literally just thinking the same exact thing."

She smiled big, and her blue eyes sparkled. "Great minds..."

"I guess so."

We walked up to the counter, and Ellie started talking to the young girl, "Good afternoon. Oh, let's see, I'm going to take the chicken wrap and a lemon drop martini."

I ordered next and got the Halcyon salad along with a chocolate espresso martini. I also ordered the tableside s'mores but asked for it to be brought out after we finished our lunch.

We sat down in the same corner booth where we'd had our first unofficial date. As we ate, Ellie began texting someone.

"Who are you texting?" I asked.

She looked up with sadness in her eyes. "Alex. She said she snuck her phone into class to ask if we were having fun."

I smiled as my heart filled with warmth. I loved Alex and Colt so damn much. Alex was so much like Ellie. I could see it already. It was too bad she was also stubborn as hell like me. Colt, on the other hand, was so laid-back that it was unreal. Hardly anything bothered that boy, except his sister.

"I told her that we are having a wonderful time together, and we are very happy." Ellie laughed and looked at me. "She just asked me if you are being romantic!"

My mouth dropped open. "How in the hell does she know what that means?"

Ellie giggled as she texted Alex back. She put her phone back in her pocket. "I told her you are probably more romantic now than when we first started dating."

The waitress came over and cleared our plates as another waitress set down the tableside s'mores.

Ellie's eyes lit up as she looked at the s'mores and then peeked up at me. "Gunner, it seems like it was just yesterday. Oh my gosh. My stomach almost feels like it's in a knot, like it was on that day."

I leaned over and gently kissed her on the lips.

"I love you, Drew Mathews."

"I love you more, Ellie Mathews. I love you so much."

I kissed her again, and I had to force myself to pull my lips from hers. "Want a s'more?"

She nodded her head in excitement as I began roasting a marshmallow.

"Gunner, do you ever think about our kids' future? Like, where do you see them at the age we were when we got married?"

My heart dropped to my stomach. "Well, shit, Ells. Considering Colt is just eight and Alex is nine, I don't even want to think that far ahead."

She giggled as she tilted her head. "Without a doubt, I see Colt wanting to run the ranch. Luke, too. Ari said that it's all he talks about."

I smiled and nodded my head. "I do see that. Even Will tells Josh that he's gonna run the ranch with the other boys."

"Alex...I see her totally being a country girl."

I shook my head. "No, I want her to live in the city for some time."

Ellie was about to put a s'more in her mouth when she stopped. "What?"

I nodded my head. "Yeah, I want her to go to college, preferably the University of Texas, and then she can spend a few years in the city."

"You mean, after college? What if she wants to be in the country?"

I shrugged my shoulders. "I just want her to have the best life possible. I could totally see her wanting to be like you," I said with a wink.

She laughed and said, "So can I."

I let out a breath. "I'm not looking forward to her liking boys, that's for damn sure."

Ellie pushed a s'more into her mouth and attempted not to smile.

My whole body sagged. "What? Does she already like boys?"

Ellie shrugged her shoulders and attempted to eat the mouthful of chocolate and marshmallow.

"Who is it? I'm gonna kill the little bastard."

Ellie slapped me and then reached for her water. "Stop it, Gunner Mathews. You're not going to put the fear in these young men when they come calling on your daughter."

"The hell I'm not."

Ellie shook her head. "What's next on our schedule?"

"I think we need to let our stomachs settle a bit and then head back to the hotel. I have a few toys to play with… thanks to Ari."

Ellie rolled her eyes and slid out from the booth as I held her hand.

"Can we go dancing tonight?" she asked.

I smiled down at my beautiful blue-eyed beauty. "Baby, we'll do whatever your little heart desires."

"Dancing. I'd love to go dancing."

I started to lead her out of Halcyon as I said, "Then, dancing it is."

Ellie and I barely made it into the hotel room before we were clawing and ripping our clothes off of each other.

"Ells, I don't think he'll work again. He's exhausted," I panted.

She let out a giggle. "Let's take a bath."

I smiled as I picked her up and carried her into the bathroom. I set Ellie down on the small bench as I began filling up the bathtub.

I started to pour some bubbles into the hot water when I heard her say, "Thank you."

I turned to see her sitting there...crying. I got up and dropped to my knees in front of her.

I pushed her hair back behind her ears and gently took her face in my hands. "Baby...please tell me those are happy tears."

She nodded her head and tried to talk.

"Yeah? They are?"

She smiled slightly as she wiped them away. "Do you remember the day we got married, and I had that panic attack? You came out and calmed me down?"

I rubbed my thumbs across her beautiful face. "Of course I remember that."

"That happened to me the first night I was here alone, and I just kept praying you would come to me."

My heart physically hurt when she spoke those words. I pulled her into my arms and sat down on the floor with her, holding her, as she cried.

"Ellie...I'm so sorry, baby. I'm so sorry. I was going crazy, trying to find you, and then Mom and Dad told me to stop after I drove around for hours. I'm sorry I didn't think about coming here. Baby, I'm so sorry. Please forgive me. God, Ellie, please don't cry."

She pulled back to look at me and smiled. "They're really not sad tears. I'm so moved by how strong our love is for each other, and if anything, I'm more upset at myself for doubting it. I need you so much, Gunner, that it scares me."

"I feel the same way."

She stood up and smiled as she walked over to the bathtub and climbed in. When she sat down, she let out a long sigh and sank until the water reached her neck. I got up and crawled in behind her. I wasn't sure how long we were in the tub, just soaking in silence. I ran my fingers along her body, and I could feel how relaxed she was.

"I think we should do this at least once a week after the kids go to bed," she said.

I chuckled. "Soak in a hot bath with my naked wife. Hell yeah."

She turned around and gave me a smoldering look as she sat on me and wrapped her legs around me.

"Not just soak in the tub...but make love in it as well."

I wasn't sure how the ole boy was keeping up, but he hadn't failed me yet. Ellie positioned herself and slowly sank down on me. She dropped her head back and moaned as she began moving slowly.

"Ellie..." I whispered.

She looked into my eyes and smiled at me.

"Faster, baby...go faster."

She picked up speed, and I felt the build happening way too fast. She placed her hands on the sides of the tub and lifted herself more before coming down harder.

"Fuck." I hissed through teeth.

The water began splashing out onto the floor, and the sound seemed to turn Ellie on even more.

"Yes. Oh God, yes. Gunner...I'm coming. I'm coming."

I dropped my head back and held off for as long as I could before it felt like I exploded inside of her. I grabbed her and pulled her body close to mine, holding her, as I poured myself into her. I never wanted this feeling to end... ever.

I spun Ellie around on the dance floor as she laughed. I knew she never got the chance to just let her hair down, so tonight, it was all about her. We danced so much that I felt like I could puke if I had to spin around one more time.

Ellie leaned in and shouted, "I think I need to leave! I'm exhausted, Gunner."

Thank God. I nodded my head and pointed to the bar. "I need a water really quick."

She smiled and grabbed my hand as we made our way to the bar. I ordered two waters, and when I handed Ellie the water, she downed the bottle in one drink. I followed and drank it down in one drink, too.

As soon as we got outside, we both sighed and then laughed. She jumped into my arms, and I spun her around.

"Jesus, I'm not cut out for this kind of stuff anymore. Sex all day and dancing all night—it's too much!"

I laughed. "I agree. My damn feet are killing me."

"Hotel?" Ellie asked.

"Yes."

By the time we got back to our hotel and showered, we were exhausted. Ellie crawled under the covers, naked, and I followed. I pulled her right up next to my body and took in everything about her—the way she smelled, the feel of her skin against mine, and her slow and steady breathing.

She's my everything. She will always be my everything. I closed my eyes and listened to her breathing become slow and steady as she drifted off to sleep.

"I love you, Ellie."

"I love you, Drew. I love you more than anything."

I smiled as I began to drift off to sleep. I dreamed of walking along the river with Ellie as we held hands, forever in love. Always.

Chapter Nine

Ellie

I OPENED MY eyes and smiled when I saw the hint of daylight shining through the curtains. I glanced over to the clock and saw it was ten thirty in the morning. I sat up quickly and searched for my phone. I grabbed it and saw a text conversation between Alex and Gunner.

> Alex: Good morning, Mama and Daddy. Colt is being a brat, but I'm excusing it since I'm sure he misses you both something awful, just like I do. You're still coming home tomorrow, right?

> Me: Hey, baby girl. It's Daddy. Smack Colt around a little bit and show him who's boss. Yes, sweetheart, we will be home tomorrow. Mommy and Daddy miss you and Colt so much, but we're having a lot of fun.

> Alex: Have you bought Mommy flowers yet?

> Me: No. Do you think I should?

Alex: Yep. Daddy, pick some off the side of the road. You know, get the daisy ones she loves so much. I think she would like that so much better. It shows you put more effort into it by picking them.

Me: When did you grow up? I'll try my best, but trying to find flowers here in Austin on the side of the road is kind of hard. It's a big city and all.

Alex: Ha-ha. I miss y'all. See you tomorrow. Kiss Mommy.

Me: I miss you and Colt, baby. See you tomorrow, and I will give Mommy a kiss.

I smiled as I set my phone down. "Gunner?" Looking toward the bathroom, I slowly got out of bed. I grinned as I felt every sore muscle in my body from the last two evenings while I made my way to the bathroom. I walked into the bathroom only to find it empty. Reaching for my robe, I put it on as I headed back out and picked up my cell phone.

Me: Where are you?

Gunner: Morning, sweetheart! Be right up!

Me: Okay. ☺

I set my phone down and walked over to the Victoria's Secret bag. There were panties, a bra, and a baby-doll nightie in the bag. I slipped the nightie on and turned to look at myself in the mirror.

"Not bad for a mom with two kids," I said as I looked at my toned body.

Of course, walking every day with Ari and Emma and working in the garden and around the ranch had contributed to much of my toned body.

I spun around, reached for the vibrator, and pulled it out. I smiled as I reached for the handcuffs and headed back to the bed. I slipped both under my pillow and lay down on the bed. I moved and pulled my leg up, trying to pull off the seductive look, but it felt awkward. Then, I turned a different way, but that felt forced. I got up on my knees, and I was about to try another position when the door opened. I looked up, and Gunner stopped dead in his tracks. I smiled and bit down on my lip as I tried my best to look sexy.

"Jesus H. Christ." Gunner shut the door. Then, he set two cups of coffee, a bag, and some flowers he had in his hand on the table. He lifted his T-shirt over his head and quickly stripped out of his jeans.

I smiled as I felt my core tighten. I began chewing on my lower lip. I was always a nervous wreck when we played like this. I wasn't sure why I enjoyed playing so much, but I was always afraid Gunner would think less of me even though he had repeated that he loved to play with vibrators on me.

He was on the bed and pushing me down before I could even say a word. His hand moved up the baby-doll nightie, and he began twisting and pulling on my nipple as he kissed me. I let out a moan as I reached my other hand under the pillow. I reached around for the handcuffs before pulling them out and holding them up.

Gunner pulled back and smiled as he took them and grabbed my left hand. He put the cuff on my left wrist and then grabbed my right hand. He looked at the headboard and made a face. He sat up and looked around. He got up and used his finger to motion for me to stand up. I stood, and he led me over to a chair.

"Sit down, Ellie, and spread your legs open...wide."

I instantly felt a rush of wetness between my legs. I did as he'd asked. He walked behind me, took my arms, and placed them behind the back of the chair. Then, he handcuffed my right hand to my left.

He walked around to the front again. "Move to the edge of the chair, baby."

I did just that, and my body clenched in anticipation for what he was about to do.

"Do you like when I make you come with my mouth, Ells?"

I nodded my head. "Yes...very much."

He dropped to his knees and pushed the chair back, causing me to let out a gasp.

"Damn, you're so beautiful." He licked his lips and held the chair back just enough to tilt me back, giving him a better angle.

When he brushed his tongue across my clit, I jumped. "Oh God."

"Yeah, baby...let me hear how good it feels."

He licked me again, and I jumped again at the feel of his tongue making a pass over my sensitive bud.

"Gunner, please don't tease me."

Then, he pushed his fingers in as he began massaging the area that he knew drove me mad.

"God, Ellie, I love making you come. I could do this all day."

He buried his mouth over my clit, and he began moving his fingers in and out as he sucked and licked me.

"Oh God. Oh God....oh God, oh God, oh God!" I called out.

I looked down, and having my hands tied and my legs spread open to him made it seem hotter.

Gunner flicked his tongue quickly against my clit and moved his fingers in and out so fast that I could feel my toes beginning to curl.

"Gunner...oh God...ah...yes...yes...I'm coming! Oh, yes!"

I cried out like a crazy person, but I couldn't help it. The orgasm ripped through my body like a tornado. I didn't want it to end. I dropped my head back and felt Gunner pull me further to the edge. He pushed the chair back more as he pushed his finger into my ass, and I fell over the edge again.

"Holy shit!" I cried out as another orgasm ripped through my body.

I opened my eyes when Gunner started taking off the cuffs. He picked me up and carried me to the bed. Once he laid me down, I reached under the pillow and pulled out the vibrator.

"Again," I whispered.

The smile that spread across Gunner's face was priceless. He turned the vibrator on and touched it to my right nipple. I jerked and held my breath as I waited for him to move it down farther. He moved it to the other side and then slowly down my stomach. I could hardly stand the wait.

When he gently pushed the vibrator inside me, he turned it on high. Within seconds, I was calling out his name.

I was flying so high from each orgasm. I could barely feel Gunner moving over me and pushing inside me. He lifted me up, and I wrapped my legs and arms around him. I leaned my forehead to his, and we just sat there. Nothing needed to be said. It was just the two of us as one.

"I love you so much, Ellie."

"I love you, too, Gunner."

I slowly began moving up and down, and I dropped my head back. The friction our bodies created when we were together was more than powerful. Gunner kissed all along my neck, whispering how much he loved me between each tender kiss.

Gunner moved and lay me down on the bed as he began to slowly and sweetly make love to me. I'd never felt so much love in my life. It was as if he was trying to tell me how much he wanted me and how much he loved me through every movement, every kiss.

I pushed my hands through his hair and arched my back when I felt him growing bigger inside me.

He placed his lips near my ear. "I'm coming, baby. Oh God...Ellie, I'm coming."

Gunner practically collapsed on top of me. He rolled over and pulled me next to him. Once our breathing slowed down, I could feel myself drifting back to sleep. I was so tired that I could hardly keep my eyes open.

"Gunner?" I whispered.

"Yeah, baby?"

"I miss the kids."

He kissed my back and said, "We'll be home by the time they get off the bus."

I smiled, closed my eyes, and slipped into a deep sleep.

I dreamed of Alex walking toward me in a beautiful white gown. *My baby girl is all grown-up.*

Chapter Ten

Gunner

AFTER SLEEPING FOR another hour, Ellie and I woke up, packed our things, and began heading back to Mason in our separate cars. I wished I would have had someone drive me to Austin, so I could be with her right now, but I used the time to make a phone call to Jeff.

"Hello?"

"Jeff, how are things going at the ranch?"

"Good. It's been pretty quiet, believe it or not. Josh stopped by and helped out with the feeding, much to Luke's disappointment."

I laughed and shook my head. "That boy is going to make one hell of a rancher someday, if he keeps it up."

Jeff chuckled. "Tell me about it. He's already told Ari and me to start saving our money because he intends on going to A&M and having at least three girlfriends."

"Ah hell, I'm sure Ari set him straight on that one."

"To be honest, I have no idea where the boy gets it from."

I let out a gruff laugh. "Yeah, right. When are you leaving for Kentucky?"

"Two days. Ari is beyond excited, and she's already packing. She almost changed her mind, but I talked her into going. I think we need some time alone."

"I'm telling you, Jeff. Do it. It's made a world of difference for Ells and me."

"I'm glad, Gunner. I'm also glad to hear you dumped that damn part-time job."

I laughed. "Yeah. Well, I thought I missed that shit, but it turns out I was missing something else."

"You douche. That's my sister, asshole."

I chuckled. "We are on our way home. I'll see you in the morning."

"Sounds good. Drive safe."

Ellie and I were sitting on the back of my tailgate when the school bus drove up. I could see Alex's and Colt's faces light up when they saw us.

Ellie let out a little, "Eep!" as she jumped off the tailgate.

When Alex stepped off the steps of the bus, she ran as fast as she could into Ellie's arms.

"Oh, Mama! I missed you so much! You look so beautiful. Did you and Daddy have fun? Y'all aren't mad at each other anymore, are you?"

My heart hurt from hearing our daughter ask that. Colt came running up, and I leaned down and caught him in my arms.

"Daddy! Uncle Jeff said I can shoot my first deer before deer season is up!"

I looked at him and smiled. "He did, huh? I'll have to talk to him about that."

Alex pulled back and allowed Colt to run into Ellie's arms.

"Mama, I missed you so much. No one makes pancakes or bacon like you do. Poor Grams just couldn't make the bacon the same, Mama. Thank goodness you're home!"

We all started laughing as Ellie stood and picked up Colt. I looked at how big our son was getting, and I felt tears building in my eyes. When I glanced down at Alex, she was watching Ellie and Colt with a smile. As much as she acted like she couldn't stand her younger brother, she loved him more than life itself. I picked her up, and she let out a small scream as I carried her to the truck.

After everyone piled into the truck, Ellie turned and looked at Alex and Colt. "It's y'all's night tonight. Dinner in? Dinner out? What do you want to do?"

I looked in the rearview mirror at Alex and Colt whispering back and forth to each other. I put the truck in drive and began making my way back to the house. I knew my kids, and I knew they would want to stay home.

Alex cleared her throat. "Colt and I would like to grill hot dogs on the fire pit and then make s'mores."

I glanced over at Ellie, and she smiled and winked at me.

"Then, I think we'd like to watch *Cars*!" Colt said with a big smile.

Ellie and I both started laughing.

I grabbed her hand and pulled it to my lips. "Do y'all know that was the first movie Mommy and I watched together? It's kind of a special movie to us."

"Really?" Alex let out a giggle. "Then, we have to watch it tonight!"

Ellie tilted her head and gave me the sweetest smile ever. "I think that sounds like the most perfect night ever."

Both kids yelled, "Yeah!"

"All right, let's head home and get homework and chores done. Then, we can plan our night."

Alex and Colt both whined and began arguing over who had to feed the dogs. I squeezed Ellie's hand as I looked at her.

She smiled as she said, "I wouldn't want it any other way."

I laughed and said, "Agreed."

By the time Colt had his fifth s'more, I was pretty sure he was going to throw up.

Ellie reached for the chocolate bars and marshmallows. "No more, young man. Now, both of y'all, go on in and get cleaned up. We'll watch *Cars* in a bit after everything is cleaned up and put away."

"Yes!" Colt yelled. He jumped up and began wiping chocolate and marshmallows on his pants.

Following him into the house, Alex said, "Colt, I will never get used to the way you eat. *Ever.* I don't care if we are old and gray and living together in an old folks' home. I will never get used to you being a pig."

"Hey! Alex, don't call your brother names!" I called out after them.

They were both in a full-blown argument and couldn't even hear me at this point.

I helped Ellie clean up. We popped some popcorn and put the *Cars* movie in. It didn't take long before both kids were sound asleep. Alex was snuggled next to me, and Colt was lying across Ellie.

I motioned to her that I was going to carry them up to their beds.

Ellie smiled, nodded her head, and mouthed, *Ka-chow*, to me.

I began laughing and wiggled my eyebrows up and down. When she nodded her head, I knew we would be sneaking off to the barn tonight.

I stood and picked up Alex. I carried her upstairs and put her in her bed.

When I covered her up, she whispered, "Daddy?"

I leaned down and kissed her on the forehead. "Yeah, sweetheart?"

"I want to marry a guy like you someday."

I felt my heart begin to slam harder in my chest. "No one will ever be good enough for my baby. No one."

She smiled. "I love you, Daddy."

"I love you more, Alexandra. I love you so much more."

I shut her door and leaned against it as I tried to contain my tears. I pushed off and made my way back downstairs to get my little man.

Colt was out for the night. He didn't even budge when I placed him in bed and covered him.

I shut his door and ran back downstairs. Ellie was in the kitchen at the back door, holding the quilt Emma had made for us for our wedding present. We only used it when we were in the barn.

"Gunner, what if one of them wakes up?"

"They won't."

She tilted her head and said, "What if?"

I walked up, grabbed her, and picked her up, and she let out a small squeal.

"Gunner..." she whispered.

I pushed the door open and made my way to the barn.

"Thank you for the last few days."

I walked into the barn and slowly set her down. I placed my hands on the sides of her face. "Thank you, Ells. Thank you for loving me, for being an amazing mother and wife, and for taking care of all of us like you do."

"Now that you have me in your barn, what are your intentions, Mr. Mathews?"

"I intend on making love to you and showing you just how much I love you. I'm going to show you how much you're wanted over and over again, Ellie."

The End

Saved

**BOOK TWO IN THE WANTED SERIES
SHORT STORY**

Chapter One

Jeff

I WALKED INTO the house and heard Ari on the phone with Heather.

"What if they get hurt? I'll be so far away. I know. I know you're right. I can't help but worry."

I smiled as I walked into the kitchen. I looked at the table and saw Luke and Grace. They were both making something with paper and crayons.

"What are y'all doing?" I asked as I pulled up a seat and sat down.

Grace looked at me and smiled. Her light brown hair and green eyes pierced mine as she smiled at me. "Daddy, we're making happy-birthday cards for Bandpa!"

I smiled as I nodded my head. I loved that my father was a huge part of our lives.

"What is that, Grace? A horse?"

She snapped her head up and looked at me. "What? No, Daddy! It's a flower vase."

I quickly glanced over to Luke, who shrugged his shoulders and smiled. I looked back down at the drawing and tried to see where in the heck she was drawing a vase.

I nodded my head. "Of course, of course. I see the vase now. I must have horses on my mind."

Grace giggled and said, "Silly, Daddy."

Ari walked up, kissed me on the cheek, and then moved her lips to my ear. "I totally saw a horse, too."

"Thank you," I said.

"Dad, can I help Uncle Gunner while you're gone?" Luke asked.

Ari sat down on my lap.

"I've already talked to him about it. Since you and Grace will be staying over there, Gunner said he will wake you up earlier to help with the feeding, if you'd like."

Luke jumped up and did a fist pump. "Yes! Yes! Dad, I swear, I'm gonna learn everything, and make you and Uncle Gunner proud some day at how well I can help with things around here."

I smiled and felt my heart growing bigger. I nodded my head. "Luke, son, you already make me proud."

"Well, don't be too proud of him just yet. Luke, you want to tell me about this dye you gave Alex to put in Colt's hair last week?"

Luke slowly sat back down and gave his mother the most innocent look ever. "Mom, I'm not to blame for that. I told Alex it wouldn't come out. She didn't believe me. I put it on Lady, and—"

Ari jumped up. "Oh my God. Is that why her tail is green? Luke Johnson, you'd better disappear from my view right now."

Luke stood and looked at me like I was going to help him out or something. I just smiled at him.

"I had to experiment on something, Mom, and Lady was—"

Ari snapped her fingers and pointed. "Luke, walk away, son, if you know what is good for you. Walk. Away."

Grace started laughing, and Luke gave her a dirty look. He turned, headed out the kitchen, and ran upstairs. I looked up at Ari, and she looked pissed.

She began shaking her head as she walked toward the stove. "Your son...I swear, I have no idea where he comes up with these ideas."

"Probably Daddy."

I glanced down at Grace and reached out to tickle her. "Daddy, huh?"

I picked her up and began swinging her around. She laughed and yelled for me to put her down.

Ari was leaning against the island, giggling. "At least we know Grace inherited my smarts."

I stopped and looked at Ari as Grace laughed even more. I put her down, walked up to Ari, and took her into my arms before kissing her.

"Yuck. That is so gross. I'm going to my room."

Grace took off up the stairs as she yelled out how no other parents kissed in front of their kids.

Ari smiled at me. "I haven't been away from them for more than two days. I'm scared."

I placed my hand on the side of her face and stared into her eyes. "We need some time alone, baby—just you and me and a few horses. They're going to be with Ellie and Gunner. My parents are here, and your parents are a phone call away. Everything is gonna be okay. We're leaving in the morning. You packed?"

She nodded her head.

I wiped away the tear rolling down her cheek. "I love you."

She leaned in and gently kissed me on the cheek. "I love you, too."

I sat in the seat next to Ari and saw that she was texting Ellie—again.

"Ari, leave her alone. You gave her a long list of things this morning, and you've called her three times already. Stop. The kids are going to be okay."

She nodded her head. "I know, I know. I can't help it though. I've never been away for so long. What if Grace thinks Ellie is a better mom? What if she never wants to come back home?"

I looked at her and then rolled my eyes. "Did you really just say that?"

She nodded her head. "I'm just tense, ya know? I've never been on a business trip with you before, and left the kids like this before. But it's been too long since I've had a mind-blowing orgasm. I'm so overdue."

The lady next to me cleared her throat, and I turned and smiled.

I looked back at Ari and leaned in closer. "Baby, I don't think the whole plane needs to hear that you're lacking in the orgasm area. Neither does my ego."

Ari turned and stared at me, and then she smiled slightly. "You have some serious making up to do."

"Is that so?"

She nodded her head and ran her tongue along the bottom of her lip. My dick jumped in my pants. If I thought I could, I would take her to the back of the plane and give her what she needed.

When the flight attendant walked by, the lady sitting next to me asked, "Are there any open seats on this flight?"

"Yes, there are some in the back. Would you like to move, ma'am?"

I looked at the lady.

She looked at me and then over toward Ari. "Yes, please."

She got up and followed the flight attendant. I instantly formed a plan in my head, and I smiled as I nodded.

Seeing the attendant walking by I held up my hand to get her attention. "Excuse me. When we get up in the air, is it possible to get a blanket?"

She smiled at me.. "I'll get you one now."

I turned back and saw Ari attempting to sneak in another text. I reached over and grabbed her phone.

"Hey! Jeff, give it back."

The flight attendant came back and handed me the blanket.

"Thank you."

"Of course. Let me know if there is anything else you need."

I grinned as I began putting the blanket over Ari while the plane backed up.

"What are you doing? I'm not cold."

"Trust me," I said as I winked at her.

Our flight was pretty empty, and no one was sitting in the seats across the aisle from us. Two people were in front of us, and from what I could tell, only two people were behind us.

The flight attendants went through the whole safety process. Ari sat there and pouted because I'd taken her phone away from her.

"You had to turn it off anyway, baby." I handed her the phone.

She leaned down, tossed it into her purse, and zipped it up. She leaned back and grabbed the blanket and pulled it up to her chin.

As the plane started taking off down the runway, I leaned over Ari and looked out the window. I slipped my hand under the blanket and began moving it under Ari's skirt. She jerked her head up as I smiled and stared straight out the window. When I reached her panties, she spread her legs open a little, and her breathing picked up. I slipped my hand down her panties and began touching her clit, moving my thumb in slow, soft circles. Ari let out a small moan and looked to see if anyone was watching. I turned and peeked at her. She bit down on her lower lip as her eyes danced with passion.

I looked back out the window as I slipped two fingers inside her. I began moving them in and out, and Ari opened her legs as much as she could.

"Holy hell," she whispered as she put her head back and closed her eyes.

My dick was getting so hard, and I needed to adjust myself, but this was for my girl. She needed an orgasm, so I was going to give her an orgasm.

I began pushing my fingers in farther. When I pushed harder on her clit, she let out a gasp and looked at me, her eyes widening, as her orgasm began. I stared into her eyes as she covered her mouth with her hand. She closed her eyes, and I could feel her squeezing down on my fingers. I leaned over, and she removed her hand from her mouth. I gently kissed her lips, as she put her hand behind my neck, pulling me closer to deepen the kiss.

When I didn't feel her squeezing around my fingers any longer, I moved my hand away. I pulled my lips from hers, and she opened her eyes. They were sparkling, and she let out a giggle as a beautiful blush covered her cheeks.

"Is that better, baby?"

"Much, much better. Thank you!"

"That's just the beginning of how this week is going to be. You won't even have a chance to worry about the kids. It's all about me and you, Ari."

She smiled bigger. "I like that plan—a lot."

Chapter Two

Ari

SCOTT HAD ARRANGED for a car to pick Jeff and me up at the airport. It was taking us to The Brown Hotel where we would be staying for the next five nights. I'd never been to Louisville, Kentucky, so this was all new to me.

After we checked in, we headed up to our suite.. The bellhop opened the door to the suite, walked in, and set our luggage down. The room was beautiful. I immediately made my way to the bathroom, and I wanted to let out a squeal when I saw the huge Jacuzzi tub. I moaned as I closed my eyes. I knew exactly what Jeff and I would be doing in there later tonight.

Jeff walked up behind me and wrapped his arms around me. "Hey, I know you're tired, baby, but I need to head out and see the horses that Scott and I are interested in."

I spun around and kissed him quickly. "Let me change into some jeans, and then I'll be ready to go. Did the car wait for us?"

"Yeah. We have him all week. I believe Scott said the driver was staying in the hotel as well. I told him to give us a few minutes, and then we would be back downstairs."

I changed and threw my hair up into a ponytail. I slipped my boots on and grabbed my jacket. It was fairly warm out but still colder than what it was in Texas.

"All right, let's go see some horses!" I was excited to head to this particular horse ranch. I'd seen pictures of the ranch, and my mouth watered at all the horses. I would love to have more horses if I thought we had the time to take care of them all.

As soon as we stepped out of the elevator, Jeff's cell phone rang. "It's Pete," he said as he hit Answer.

"Pete, how are you? Yes, the flight was great." Jeff looked at me and raised his eyebrows.

I felt the blush move across my cheeks.

"We're heading that way now. Yes, the driver has the address. Looking forward to it, Pete. See ya soon." Jeff hit End and smiled at me.

The driver opened the door for us, and we both slipped into the car.

As we drove farther out of the city, the countryside grew more beautiful.

I let out a gasp and said, "Jesus H. Christ, look at these ranches. They're huge. It's beautiful here."

There wasn't any snow on the ground since it had been so warm, and everything seemed to be green, like it was spring.

The driver pulled into a driveway, and I couldn't help but notice the sign—*Notting Hill Ranch*.

The driver hit a button and gave our names. Moments later the massive black iron gates opened. We began driving down the driveway, and on both sides was a six-plank white fence. Horses were scattered throughout the pastures, and my heart was pounding faster and faster as we got closer. There was nothing I loved more—besides Jeff and my children—than horses.

"Pete said he has the two horses ready if you want to go for a ride," Jeff said.

I nodded my head in excitement.

The driver pulled up and parked next to a truck with a guy standing against it. He smiled and waved quickly. Jeff got out, turned, and reached his hand for mine to help me out.

"Jeff, Ari, it's a real pleasure."

"Pete, how are you? It's nice to finally meet you in person," Jeff said as he reached his hand out to shake Pete's.

"Yes, sir, it is. Welcome to our little slice of heaven."

I looked around and smiled. It sure was heaven. "It's breathtaking here. The hills are just beautiful. I can only imagine how it looks with snow on them."

Pete let out a small laugh. "It's beyond beautiful. Let's head to the barn."

Jeff and Pete began walking, and I followed behind them. I wanted to take everything in. I wanted to know how they managed everything, how their barns were set up, how they ran the day-to-day operations of the farm. We walked into the barn, and I let out a gasp.

"Oh. My. God," I whispered.

The first thing I noticed was the gray brick floor. Then, my eyes moved up to the stalls. They were gorgeous. The bottom part looked to be oak plank doors, and the top was a black metal mesh.

When my eyes kept moving up. "Holy hell."

The barrel ceiling was cedar planks and absolutely breathtaking. *This damn barn was nicer than our house.*

"Ari..."

I snapped my head forward and looked at Jeff. He motioned for me to follow them to the other side of the barn.

"I take it you like our barn, Ari?" Pete said with a chuckle.

It wasn't lost on me how this guy kept looking down at my legs and then my chest. *Jerk.* "Like it? I want to move into it. Is it heated in the winter?"

Pete blushed.

"No freaking way!" I laughed.

"My babies are spoiled, but they make me good money."

When we stepped outside the barn, my eyes looked upon two of the most beautiful men I'd ever seen. Nothing but muscles...lean muscles with bodies built for endurance. My heart began pounding, and I was pretty sure I let out a moan.

"Ari, Jeff, I'd like you to meet Sweet Dancer and My Fair Charmer."

I walked up to Sweet Dancer and looked into his eyes. Those beautiful brown eyes immediately captivated me.

I want him. I must have him.

"I'm riding Sweet Dancer," I said before Jeff could claim him.

Sweet Dancer had to be at least two hands taller than My Fair Charmer. He was beyond perfect.

Jeff let out a chuckle.

"Ari, are you okay with an English saddle?" Pete asked.

I smiled. "I learned on an English saddle, so yes, I'm perfectly fine with that."

Pete laughed and looked at Jeff.

Jeff raised his hands and said, "I might look rough and tough, but I have a softer side. I've ridden English plenty of times."

Pete grinned. "Perfect. Well, they're all saddled up. I think Sweet Dancer here is going to give Charmer a run for his money."

I put my foot in the stirrup and got myself seated on top of my new boyfriend. *Oh yeah, he feels good between the legs.*

I glanced over to Jeff, and he was sitting on top of My Fair Charmer, just staring at me with a smirk on his face. I smiled, and he winked.

"If you get lost, don't worry. They'll bring ya back. Charmer here will do anything for oats, and it's about time for his midday snack."

Jeff and I started the horses off toward a trail as Pete yelled out for us to have fun.

I turned and yelled back, "Oh, we will! Trust me!"

We rode along in silence as Jeff checked out each horse. Once we came up to an open field, I peeked over at Jeff, and he started laughing.

"Turn him loose, baby."

All I had to do was give the horse a small amount of leg pressure, and he took off. I could not believe how fast this horse could go. I hadn't felt so free in my life. If given the chance, I was pretty sure he would just keep on running. I slowed him down, and we began turning around. I wasn't even sure how far I had let the horse run until I saw Jeff running toward us. He slowed Charmer down and trotted up to me. The smile on his face caused me to smile bigger.

"How did he feel?"

"Amazing. His power and speed is crazy. I fell in love with him the moment I crawled on top of him. "

Jeff lifted the corner of his mouth. "I'd say. It looked like you were about to have an orgasm when you crawled on top of him."

"I about did."

Jeff threw his head back and laughed. Sweet Dancer was probably one of the best behaved horses I'd ever been on. I smiled as my evil little plan began playing out. I looked around and started to head to a group of trees. I was hoping that somewhere within the group of trees was an open field.

Jeff followed me as I took Sweet Dancer on a little adventure hike. Just a few feet in, I spied what I was looking for—a small pasture surrounded by nothing but trees. I walked to the middle of it and turned the horse around.

"Um...what are you doing, Ari?"

I reached down and pulled my sweatshirt and T-shirt up and over my head at the same time. I dropped them to the ground, and I instantly felt my nipples getting harder from the cool breeze.

"Baby...what are you doing?"

I stood up on the stirrups and unbuttoned my pants before taking off my jeans. How I managed to get my jeans and panties off while staying on the horse was a miracle in itself.

"Jesus, are you trying to kill me?"

I turned around on Sweet Dancer, moved off the saddle, and motioned for Jeff to get up on the horse. I'd never seen him move so fast in my life. He kicked his boots off and stripped out of his jeans. Then, he quickly got up on Sweet Dancer and sat on the saddle facing me.

"I've always wanted to have sex on a horse."

"I just fucking died and gone to heaven, Ari."

I giggled as I reached down and began stroking his dick. I licked my lips as I looked down at it. I placed my legs on Jeff's and moved myself closer to him. I sat up and slowly began to sink down onto him. I dropped my head back as he filled every inch of me.

"Damn it...Ari, you feel so good."

I used my leg muscles to start moving up and down while Jeff held on to Sweet Dancer's reins. The horse never moved a muscle while I began rode him faster. Jeff started moving along with me, meeting me thrust for thrust.

"Jeff...oh God, yes."

"Ah...baby...faster. Come on, baby...faster, harder, Ari."

"Yes. Oh God, yes." I dropped my head back as I felt the build.

Jeff pushed my bra up, exposing my breasts to him. When he began sucking on my nipple, I lost it.

"Yes! Yes! Oh God, yes! I'm coming, Jeff...oh God."

My orgasm seemed to last forever. I'd never enjoyed sex so much in my life. When I came down from my orgasm and looked at Jeff, he was smiling at me.

"Turn around, baby."

Somehow, I managed to turn around without falling off the horse. Jeff pushed me down and lifted me some. Before I could even get ready for him, he slammed into me, causing me to yell out. He grabbed my hips and began moving.

"Ari...you...drive...me...crazy. You feel so damn good."

After a few more times of Jeff moving in and out, deep and hard, we began calling out each other's names. My legs were weak, and my damn stomach muscles were cramping. I turned around carefully and wrapped my legs around Jeff. He was still a bit hard, so I began rubbing against him.

"That feels so good," I whispered. I wasn't sure why I was still so horny after two amazing orgasms. "Jeff, I want more."

"Damn, Ari. Baby, that was hot as hell, but I don't think he will come up that fast. Ah shit. I think I got cum on the saddle."

I pulled back and looked at him. I frowned that he was more worried about that than making me feel good. I began grinding against him as I bit down on my lower lip.

He shook his head. "Nope, not gonna happen. The old boy won't be ready for at least another hour."

The friction from Jeff's semihard dick and the saddle against my skin was causing another buildup.

"Jeff, oh God...I'm going to come again." I ground against him faster as it rubbed my clit in just the right way.

"Ari, baby...my leg is cramping. I need you to move!"

I shook my head. "No...oh God, I'm going to come again. Don't move."

He moved.

He must have pressed against Sweet Dancer because the damn horse began to take off. The next thing I knew, Jeff and I were on the ground and damn near naked.

I turned to see Sweet Dancer running off through the trees, and lo and behold, My Fair Charmer followed him. Jeff jumped up and began running after them. I lost it, laughing. Seeing my half-naked husband running with no boots and free as a bird was a moment I would never forget.

"Fucking son of a bitch!" Jeff yelled. He turned and began walking back.

He must have noticed that he didn't have any shoes on because he started hopping while bitching about sticks and rocks. I quickly put on my T-shirt, sweatshirt, and jeans. I slipped my boots on and walked toward the trees. Jeff was attempting to put his jeans on while jumping around on one foot. I let out a whistle, and Jeff laughed.

"You heard what Pete said. They'll head back to the barn. Shit. We need to start walking and come up with a story as to how we let two twenty-five thousand dollar racehorses get away from us."

I stoppedwalking. "Me? Why do I have to come up with a story?"

"Because you wanted to have sex on the horse, that's why." He dropped his head back and mumbled something.

"What did you say?"

He looked at me and said, "What if there is cum on the saddle? Oh God. Scott is gonna kill me."

I just stood there and stared at him. "Really? That's what you're worried about. We just had mind-blowing sex on a horse, which took off and left us to walk God knows how many miles back, and you're worried about cum possibly being on the saddle?"

He shrugged his shoulders. "Yeah."

I stepped out of the trees and smiled. Sweet Dancer and My Fair Charmer were both grazing in the open field. I let out a whistle, and Dancer looked up. The moment he saw me, he came trotting over. He stopped just short of me and nudged his nose against my shoulder. I grabbed on to his reins.

When I turned and looked at Jeff, I smiled bigger. "I think he likes me."

Jeff shook his head and started walking out to get My Fair Charmer.

Dancer started whinnying a bit, and I began moving my hands down his neck.

"Shh...don't worry, baby. You'll grow to love him, just like I did."

Chapter Three

Jeff

ARI AND I talked about Sweet Dancer and My Fair Charmer as we rode back to the main barn.

"Are you and Scott thinking about breeding only or racing as well?"

"After seeing Sweet Dancer take off, I think he needs to be racing."

Ari nodded her head. "I agree, but I don't want to send him off somewhere here for training. I want to take him back to Texas. I think you should call Layton Morris in Llano. Y'all have worked together a few times. His trainer, Lucky, is damn good."

Layton Morris and Reed Moore were two great guys that we had worked with both on the horse side of things and the cattle side. "Yeah, Layton is a good guy. Scott and Gunner really like him and Reed. That's a good idea, Ari."

When the barn came into view, My Fair Charmer picked up his pace, and I laughed as I patted him on the neck. "What about this guy?"

Ari giggled. "I think he is a keeper. I'd like to look at

his bloodline though. He seemed fast, but I'm thinking we could stud him out."

Ari and I both came to a stop as two young boys walked up. After we got down, the boys took both horses.

Pete walked up. "Well? Did you enjoy yourself?"

My dick jumped as an image of Ari fucking me on the horse popped into my head. I quickly peeked over to Ari, who turned and then began following the boys.

I smiled and nodded my head. "We did. Both horses are fast, really fast. Ari wants to take a look at My Fair Charmer's bloodline. We already looked at Sweet Dancer's on the plane."

Pete smiled. "Sure. Let's head on back to the house and go to my office. I've already got info for both horses for y'all."

I glanced over and saw Ari brushing Sweet Dancer as he bobbed his head up and down. That damn horse had fallen in love with her as fast as she had with him.

"I take it your wife likes Sweet Dancer," Pete said with a chuckle.

I looked back at him. "I wouldn't be surprised if she wanted to sleep in his stall with him tonight."

Pete laughed and slapped me on the back. "Time to get out the checkbook, my boy."

I rolled my eyes. "Not much room for negotiation, is there?"

"Not with that horse."

"Let me grab Ari. Excuse me, Pete." I walked over to Ari and wrapped my arms around her. "When we get home, I want a repeat of this afternoon."

She handed the brush in her hand to one of the young boys, and then she turned around in my arms. "That, my dear, is one thing I am certainly going to agree with you on."

"Come on. Pete wants us to meet him in his office."

Three hours later, Ari and I were back at the hotel. We were changing clothes to meet Pete and his girlfriend for dinner. Ari walked out of the bathroom in a beautiful black cocktail dress that showed off her curves.

"You look stunning," I said.

She smiled and did a little turnaround.

The moment I saw the back, my smile disappeared, and my mouth dropped open. "Oh, hell no. No. You have to wear something else."

Her smile faded, and she put her hands on her hips. "After all these years, do you really think you can tell me what to wear, Jeff Johnson? I like this dress. It makes me feel sexy."

"It damn near goes down to your ass crack."

Ari rolled her eyes. "No, it doesn't."

"Yeah, it does. Did you bring another dress?"

She looked at me like I was stupid. "Of course I did. Do you really want me to change?"

"Please."

She turned and stormed away before slamming the bathroom door. I let out a sigh and shook my head. The evening was not starting out how I'd wanted. I knew we were both tired from flying in early and then the afternoon at the horse farm. We just needed to make it through this evening with Pete. I had already gotten him to lower the price on My Fair Charmer. I just needed to work him down lower on Sweet Dancer.

I sat down and ran my hand through my hair. Something about Pete wasn't sitting right with me. The way he'd kept looking at Ari was starting to piss me off. If it were just she and I going out to dinner, I wouldn't have cared about the dress.

The bathroom door opened, and Ari came walking out. My mouth dropped open. She was wearing a black lace push-up bra with matching lace panties. She walked over to the dresser and pulled out tan sheer hose and a garter belt. She put on the garter belt, and then she placed her right foot on the end of the bed. She began slipping on the sheer hose. She moved them up her leg in a way that had my dick getting harder by the second. She clipped the garter to the hose and repeated the whole process with her left leg. I swallowed hard and licked my lips.

She turned and walked to the closet, opened it, and stood there. She reached in for another black dress and took it off the hanger. When she turned around, she glared at me as she began to put the dress on. It was another beautiful dress. It showed off her cleavage and had a slit that came up just a bit on the right side.

I stood up and said, "You look beautiful, Ari."

She didn't say a word as she walked over and slipped on her heels. She reached down, grabbed her clutch, and turned once more to look at her hair. She spun around and began toward the door. "We're running behind now."

She threw the door open and walked out of the room while I stood there, trying to get my dick to go back down. I shook my head to clear the image of me taking her in the elevator.

I made my way next to her in front of the elevator, and I looked down at her. "Ari, don't be—"

The doors opened, and Pete and his girlfriend were standing inside the elevator. I took one look at the girl and how she was dressed, and I knew Ari was going to be pissed. The girl couldn't have been older than twenty-one, twenty-two tops, and she was dressed in a red cocktail dress. It was so short that if she turned around, I was sure I would see her ass cheeks hanging out.

"Jeff, Ari, we were just coming up to get you. Are y'all ready to head to dinner?" Pete asked.

"Sorry. I had a problem with the dress I was wearing," Ari said as she stepped into the elevator.

I watched as Pete looked Ari up and down. I balled my hands into fists when he let his eyes roam a little too long on her chest. The young girl walked up, held her hand out to Ari, and introduced herself as Candy. After one look at the girl's back, I closed my eyes and shook my head before opening my eyes again.

Fuck me.

Ari was going to be pissed at me. The girl's dress exposed her bare back all the way down, except I could actually see the top of her ass crack. I quickly looked up, and Ari was shooting daggers at me.

Son of a bitch.

She'd just caught me checking out this girl, but I hadn't really checked her out.

Did I? Shit. This is going to be a long night.

By the time we walked into the restaurant, the tension between Ari and me had grown more and more. Pete had picked some fancy French restaurant, and as soon as he'd found out that Ari spoke French, the two of them continued speaking in French.

After being led to our table, we took our seats. I was sitting across from Pete, Ari was to my left, and Candy was to my right. I wanted to roll my eyes every time Pete called her Candy Cane.

"My French isn't as good as Ari's, so maybe we could stick with English?" I said as I glared at Pete.

He started laughing.

It was the longest dinner of my life. Candy kept reaching over and touching my hand. I finally ended up keeping it on my leg. If she licked her lips one more time, I was going to offer her Chapstick. I glanced over to Ari. She was smiling at something Pete had said. When she turned to me, her smile faded as she glared at me.

"Jeff, show me what a real Texas cowboy feels like on the dance floor."

I looked at Candy and then back at Ari, before turning back to Candy. "I'm not much into dancing. I'm sure Pete would love to dance with you though."

Pete stood up, and to my surprise, he reached for Ari's hand. "Nonsense. Ari, my dear, dance with me while your husband takes Candy for a spin on the dance floor."

I was sure Ari would say no.

But then, she jumped up and said, "Sounds like a plan. You can tell me more about Sweet Dancer, and I'll be able to see if you're a sweet dancer as well."

My mouth dropped open, and Pete started laughing. I watched them both walk out to the dance floor. He took her into his arms, and they began dancing. A few times, Ari threw her head back and laughed at something the dickhead had said to her.

I jumped when I felt Candy place her hand on my leg.

She began to move it up toward my dick. "Looks like they're occupied. We could sneak off somewhere."

I pushed her hand off of me. "No, thanks."

When she placed her hand on my leg again, I stood up. I looked out and saw Ari's body pressed up against Pete's. She was just a little too close to him. I moved over and sat down in Ari's seat to get away from Candy. I glanced over at Candy, and she pouted as I sat back. I let out a sigh and turned back to my wife as she danced in the arms of another man. When she glanced at me, she seemed surprised that I was sitting in her seat, and then she backed away a little from Pete.

Oh, did you realize how fucking close you were to him, Ari?

Pete said something to Ari that caused her to look back at him, and she laughed again. I stood up and pushed my chair back. I reached for my wallet, grabbed a handful of money, and threw it on the table.

"Tell Ari I took a taxi back to the hotel. All of a sudden, I feel sick to my stomach." I turned and walked away before Candy could say anything.

The moment the cool night air hit my face, I felt like I could breathe again.

I can't believe she would dance with a guy like that. Hell, I can't believe she danced with him at all.

I hailed for a taxi, but it kept driving on. I stepped a little closer to the street and hailed another. When it pulled over, I opened the door and got in. I went to close the door, but someone jerked it back open. I looked out, and Ari was standing there.

"Where are you going?" she said as she panted for breath.

"He got ya so worked up that you can't breathe?"

She looked at me funny and then gave me a dirty look. "No. When I saw you were gone, I walked back to the table, and Candy Cane said you left. I grabbed my clutch and ran out of the restaurant. Why in the hell would you leave me there?"

"Looked like you were having fun." I turned and told the driver, "The Brown Hotel, please."

Ari began getting into the taxi. I slid over and looked out the window. Neither one of us said a word to each other. The taxi driver tried to make small talk. Our answers were one-worded replies until he finally gave up.

He pulled up to the front of the hotel, and I handed him some money.

"Keep the change. Thank you, and have a great evening."

"Thank you, sir. You do the same."

Ari was out of the taxi and almost through the entrance doors of the hotel by the time I stepped out of the taxi. I smiled and nodded at the doorman as I walked through. I was suddenly overcome with exhaustion. I walked up and stood next to Ari.

"I get that you were pissed at me, Ari, but I don't know why you would dance with him. Then, you let him hold you so close. I would never do something like that to you."

She didn't say a word. The elevator door opened, and we both stepped inside.

When the door shut, she turned and looked at me. "You didn't seem to have a problem with her dress. Why is that, Jeff? You were staring pretty hard."

I knew it. "Jesus, Ari. She walked right the fuck in front of me, and when I saw the back of it, I knew you were going to be pissed. I didn't want you to wear that damn dress because Pete had been eye-fucking you all day. The last thing I wanted was for him to see you in such a sexy dress. I can't even imagine if he had danced with you while you wore that dress and if he touched your bare skin..." I turned away from her because I was getting pissed as I thought about her being in his arms.

The elevator door opened, and I stormed out. I walked to our room, and turned to see Ari was slowly making her way behind me. I opened the door and held it for her.

"Thank you," she whispered as she stepped in and stood there.

I moved around her, and began taking off my tie and then jacket. I didn't even have the energy to take a shower. I stripped out of all my clothes and crawled into bed.

"Jeff, I didn't—"

"I'm tired, Ari. I don't feel like talking. I just want to go to sleep."

I knew I was being a douche, but for some reason, I wanted her to know how much she'd hurt me by dancing with that fucker. Tomorrow, I would write him a check for full price on both horses and change out the plane tickets.

The only thing I wanted right now was to be home.

Chapter Four

Ari

I LAY IN bed and listened to Jeff's breathing. He had fallen asleep within minutes of lying down. I closed my eyes and cursed myself for dancing with that dickhead. I knew he had been eyeing me all day, and when Candy had asked Jeff to dance, he would turn her down.

Shit. Shit. Shit.

I thought back to when I had seen Jeff sitting in my seat. Candy must have come on to him, and that was why he'd moved. That was when I'd realized how close I was to Pete, and I'd backed away. Jeff had looked at me, and I could see the hurt all over his face. Pete had made a joke, and I'd looked back at him and laughed. I had asked one question about Sweet Dreamer before turning to see that Jeff had left. I had immediately walked off the dance floor and asked Candy where Jeff went. I had never run so fast in my life while wearing heels, but I'd had to get to him before he left. I hadn't even said good-bye to Pete or Candy.

I needed to do something to make up for what I had done to Jeff. I decided I would think of something in the morning, and I drifted off to sleep.

I rolled over, opened my eyes, and yawned. I reached for Jeff, but all I felt was empty space.

"I'm about to call and change our tickets to go home today."

I sat up quickly and looked at Jeff. He was standing at the window, looking out over the Ohio River.

"What?" I yelled out.

Jeff turned and looked at me.

I jumped out of bed and grabbed my robe. "I don't want to go home. We have five days. You said we had five days!" I shouted.

"Hey, Scott, can I call you back? Yeah, I'm meeting him in the lobby in about an hour to pay him. Yeah, by tomorrow, I hope. Let me call you back."

I placed my hands on my hips. There was no way in hell I was going home early. We hardly ever got alone time. I still had four days left.

"Ari, I think it's best if we just head home."

My mouth dropped open. My heart broke in two because he wanted to go home, and then I quickly moved on to being pissed.

"Grow up, Johnson. I made a fucking bad call when I danced with that douche last night. I tried to tell you I was sorry last night, but you wouldn't even let me talk. You didn't even give me a chance to say that I'd acted like a child and I was sorry. You just up and decided that we don't deserve to be alone together. Is that it? So, because I danced with a guy last night, you have decided that you're going to sulk. Well, I'm sorry, but that is not happening. What happened between us yesterday afternoon was amazing. I haven't felt like that in a very long time. I forgot what it was like to have passionate hot sex and to do wild and crazy things. I don't want that to be it. I don't want to go back to Texas with us not talking to each other because we're mad. We'll get home and just bury it all, and then we'll go back to our everyday life. I don't want that."

When I began crying, Jeff took a step toward me, but I stepped back, and he stopped.

"I want us, Jeff. I want to just be with you. I want to spend the next four days laughing, making love, shopping, making love...and maybe more shopping."

Jeff just stared at me, and a sob escaped my mouth.

"Damn it. You're not pushing me away because of one stupid, meaningless fucking dance! The only pushing you're allowed to do is with me up against a wall while you're fucking me."

Jeff dropped his cell phone to the floor and quickly walked up to me. He grabbed me and picked me up as I wrapped my legs around him. He slammed his lips to mine, and we began kissing each other like it was our last kiss. He slammed me against the wall and held me up as he tried to unbutton his pants. I moved my hands and helped him push his pants and underwear down. When his erection sprang free, I let out a moan.

I looked into his eyes and whispered, "I need my husband to fuck me—now."

Jeff gave me his smile that made my heart melt.

He whispered, "I love you, Ari."

"I love you, too."

"Now is not the time to be gentle though, baby."

He pushed open my robe and began sucking on a nipple as I grabbed on to his shoulders. He quickly pushed himself into me and began fucking me hard and fast. It was exactly what we'd both needed. We couldn't do this kind of thing at home anymore, and to just let go and not try to be quiet was an unbelievable feeling.

"Harder, Jeff! Harder!"

He held on to me tighter and walked us over to the bed, never once pulling out of me. He dropped me onto the bed, and I let out a squeal. I could feel my stomach clenching from the way he was looking at me.

"Please, Jeff...please."

"Move up, Ari, and grab the headboard."

I scurried as fast as I could and grabbed the headboard.

"I'm going to fuck you, baby. Don't let go of the headboard."

I nodded my head. He slowly pushed into me and then pulled almost all the way out. I wanted to scream for him to go faster. He did it two more times, and I began thrashing my head back and forth.

"Jeff!"

He gave me a smirk and said, "You just feel so good, so damn warm."

"Fuck me already!"

He pushed into me so hard and deep that I was shocked I hadn't come on the spot. He dug into my hips and gave me exactly what I had asked for.

I felt the buildup beginning, and I screamed out, "Harder. Damn it! Harder!"

Our bodies slapped together, making the sexiest noises I'd ever heard.

"Ari...baby, I'm getting close."

Then, it hit me. I started calling out his name over and over. "Jeff, I'm coming! Yes! Oh, yes! Jeff, harder!"

It didn't take long before Jeff called out my name. He collapsed on top of me while panting for air. He rolled over, and we both lay there, desperately gasping for air.

"Jesus, Mary, and Joseph. I. Can't. Breathe, Jeff."

"My. God. You're. Amazing. Do you know that?"

I let out a giggle as Jeff sucked in air. I rolled over and lightly moved my finger around in circles on his chest.

"I like being fucked by you," I said.

His head snapped over to me. "And I like fucking you—a lot."

I smiled as I crawled on top of him. I leaned down and placed my hands on his chest. "Then, do it more often."

His eyes filled with lust, and he nodded his head.

It wasn't often I could cause him to be silent, so I took in the moment and enjoyed it thoroughly.

Chapter Five

Jeff

ARI AND I walked together, holding hands, as we window-shopped at all the little stores downtown. I was still flying high from our little round of lovemaking this morning, and by the glow on Ari's face, I thought it was safe to think she was, too.

"I'm kind of getting hungry. Are you ready for lunch?" I asked.

She nodded her head. "Yes. I didn't even realize how hungry I was until you said something!"

I saw a little café. "How about that place?" I pointed up ahead.

She turned and looked. "Perfect!"

We walked up to the hostess, and she quickly seated us on the patio.

Ari wrapped her arms around herself and began rubbing her arms.

"Are you chilly?

She smiled. "Just a little, but I'm okay."

I stood up, took off my jacket, and handed it to her. "Here, babe. I have a T-shirt under my long-sleeved shirt."

Ari gave me that adorable smile of hers where she scrunches up her nose and her eyes gleam with happiness. "Are you sure?"

I nodded my head as I walked around the table, and I helped her put it on. As I sat back down, I thanked God that Ari had made us stay. This whole morning and afternoon had been amazing.

The waitress took our drink order and gave us a few minutes to look at the menu.

I peeked up and let out a chuckle when I saw Ari looking at me. "What are you thinking about?"

She shrugged. "You. Us. How much I love you and how happy you make me."

"I love you, too, baby, and you've always made me so happy, Arianna. I don't know what I would do if I didn't have you in my life."

She glanced back down at the menu and then said, "I know what I want—a big cheeseburger with french fries... or maybe onion rings instead. Yeah, I want onion rings for sure."

"You wanna split the onion rings?" I asked.

When she didn't respond, I looked up.

"Really? Do you not know me at all? Onion rings, Jeff. Onion. Rings. No, I'm not sharing them with you."

I dropped the menu and held up my hands. "Hey, the mind-blowing sex this morning must have screwed with my brain. I forgot how much you love them."

Ari laughed. "I'd say. I think I might like a repeat of that mind-blowing sex this afternoon, if you're, um...up for it."

I grinned. "I'm in the mood for more, screw-with-my-head sex for sure. We could even try—" For some reason, I looked up and over Ari's shoulder, and I instantly stopped talking.

You have got to be kidding me. What in the hell is he doing here?

Ari kicked me under the table and leaned forward. "What's wrong? Just the thought of you being inside—ouch! Why in the hell did you kick me?"

I jerked my head and motioned for Ari to turn around.

She looked at me with a confused look, and then she turned and jumped up. "Daddy? Oh my gosh! What are you doing here?"

Mark glared at me as Ari wrapped her arms around her father. She pulled back and asked him again, "Daddy, why in the world are you here in Kentucky?"

When he finally stopped shooting daggers at me, he looked at Ari and smiled. "Your mother and I are in town for a Fragile X auction. A dear friend of mine from college is hosting the auction."

"When's the auction? Is it open to the public? Why didn't y'all tell me about it? I swear, I told Mom that Jeff and I were going out of town."

Mark snapped his eyes back at me, and I slid a little further down in my seat. The man still scared the shit out of me, and I was pretty sure his threat of knowing people who knew people had been spot-on.

"It's tonight. It's invite only, but I'm sure Jason wouldn't mind at all if my daughter and her"—I smiled as he looked at me and shook his head—"husband came along as our guests. It's a formal dinner and a dance afterward."

Ari did that little jump she would do when she was excited. She clapped her hands and turned to me. "Shopping!"

I gave her a grin and began looking around for our waitress. I needed to put someone else between Mark and me.

As our waitress walked up, Ari quickly gave her father a kiss. "Plan on us being there for sure. I'll call Mom here in a bit."

Mark smiled warmly at Ari as he leaned down and gave her a kiss. He looked over at me as I stood up and he reached his hand out for mine.

"Mark, it was great to see you."

He looked me up and down and frowned before giving me a smile. "You, too. Enjoy the rest of your afternoon... shopping."

I quickly sat back down and swallowed hard as Ari giggled. When Mark turned and walked away, I felt like I could breathe again. I leaned back in the chair and looked up at our waitress, who had been waiting patiently.

"I need a drink, a very large drink," I said.

"He does not. Don't listen to him. I'll have the cheeseburger, well-done with everything, um...and an order of onion rings with ranch dressing on the side, please."

Ari tilted her head and smiled at me. I had no idea how she could recover so fast from all that.

"I'll take what she ordered."

The waitress laughed and took our menus. "Let me know if you change your mind about that drink."

I nodded and mumbled, "I will."

"Oh my gosh. We get to go to a formal dinner and dance tonight. How exciting! Maybe we could get a few leads on some horses tonight." Ari sat back and began twisting her hair with her finger.

She only did that when she was nervous.

Aha! So, her dad overhearing us did bother her. I knew it! "Does it not bother you at all that your dad—yet again—walked up on us talking about sex? And not just normal sex but mind-blowing, hot sex."

Ari shrugged. "Nah. I'm pretty sure he knows we have sex. He has two grandchildren."

I shook my head. "Not the same thing, Ari. Not the same thing."

She pulled out her phone and waved her hand at me like she wanted to brush the conversation away.

Fine by me. I'd be the one who dealt with her dad and his death stare all night long.

"Let me find a dress store. Oh! There's one right around the corner. We'll have to rent you a tux." She looked at me through her eyelashes and bit down on her lip. "Oh God, I get so turned-on when you're in a tux."

I smiled and felt my dick come to attention. "Oh, yeah?"

She nodded her head. "Oh, yeah, very much so."

I wiggled my eyebrows up and down.

Ari let out a little moan. "Mr. Johnson, I'm going to get a dress that will knock you out of your damn boots."

I adjusted my tux in the mirror and ran my hand through my hair to give it that perfect look. Ari was still getting ready. She wouldn't let me see the dress she had bought earlier today, and she'd kept teasing me with hints about it.

The bathroom door opened slowly, and I held my breath. When she opened the door completely, I exhaled quickly. I was pretty sure my mouth was hanging open.

Ari stood before me in a beautiful ivory strapless gown that was covered in lace. The slit on the side went far up her leg. I almost wanted to tell her she had to take the dress off and put something else on. I moved my eyes up and saw the diamond necklace with the matching diamond drop earrings. I had bought them for her for our five-year anniversary. Her hair was pulled up with just a few curls framing her face. Her bright-red lipstick made it seem like she had just stepped out of a movie set from the 1950s. My eyes wandered back down her body before landing on her perfect chest.

"I'm pretty sure this push-up bra has my breasts up to my chin. What do you think?" she asked.

I licked my lips as I slowly shook my head. "You take my breath away."

She smiled bigger and bit down on her lower lip. She ran her finger up and down her exposed thigh and said, "Easy access for you, my dear."

"Hell yeah, it is."

The phone in the room rang, and I walked over to pick it up. "Hello? Okay, we're heading down right now."

I looked at Ari as I hung up the phone. She nodded as she grabbed her clutch.

Ari and I made our way to the elevator, and I pushed the button for the ground floor.

Right as the doors opened in the lobby, Ari started to walk out of the elevator. "I'm not wearing any panties."

My heart dropped, and I had to hold on to the wall to steady myself. I watched as she retreated away from me. "Fuck. This is going to be a long night."

I held Ari close to me as we danced. I couldn't help but think back to the first time I ever held her in my arms. I pulled her closer to me so that she could see how much I needed her.

"Mr. Johnson, do you want to have a little fun?"

Smirking, I said, "Don't tease. It's not nice, Mrs. Johnson. My dick has been hard ever since you told me your little secret as you walked off the elevator."

Ari attempted to play innocent. "Little secret? I don't know what you mean by that."

"Really? Should I slip my hand under your dress to see if you were telling the truth?"

Her eyes lit up, and an evil grin spread across her face. "If you think you can slip your hand under my dress with my father somewhere in this room just to see if I'm sans panties, you go right ahead."

I let out a gruff laugh. "Baby, I'd have sex with you right here, right now. I'm not afraid of your father."

Ari grinned. "Uh-huh, sure you would."

She quickly darted her eyes around the dance floor. The lights had been dimmed after dinner.

"I'll tell you what. If you have the courage to check for panties, I'll have sex with you somewhere in this building."

I swallowed hard. The idea thrilled me...and scared the piss out of me. I quickly began looking around.

Where could I take her so that no one could see?

Bathroom?

No, too public.

The hallway out back.

I had accidentally walked out the wrong door earlier looking for the restroom, and it led to the service hallway. I smiled, knowing I was going to bury my dick deep inside my wife within the next few minutes.

I spun her around and danced our way off to the side and toward the back corner.

"You really think you've got it in you?" she asked with the most beautiful smile ever.

I slowly moved my hand down her bare back and to her leg. She jumped when I pushed my hand up and under her dress, and I quickly found my way to heaven. When I brushed my fingers across her lips, we both let out a moan.

"Son of a bitch, Ari."

She smiled bigger. "Where are you thinking, Mr. Johnson?"

I quickly pulled my hand out before anyone could see what I had been doing.

I grabbed her hand and began walking toward the door leading out to the service hallway. "Let's go. I'm going to explode."

"Ari? Ari, darling."

Ari pushed against my back, moving me forward. "No. Keep walking. Don't look back!"

"Ari, Sue is gonna see where we're going!"

"Keep moving!"

"Ari! Arianna Johnson."

Sue was not about to let Ari get away. I stopped, and Ari let out a sigh.

She put a smile on her face and slowly turned around. "Yes, Mama?"

Sue smiled and motioned for us to come to her. "Ari, Jeff, I'd like you to meet John and Trixie Donovan. John is your father's good friend. They met in college."

Ari shook hands with John and then Trixie. "It's a pleasure to meet you," Ari said.

I repeated the gesture.

Trixie smiled as she grabbed Ari's arm and began walking her over to a table. Ari looked over her shoulder at me, and I shrugged. I followed John as he began asking me what had brought us to Kentucky.

Before I knew it, we were all sitting at our table, and John and I were laughing and exchanging stories. I glanced over at Ari. She was attempting to appear to be interested in the conversation with Trixie, but she clearly wasn't. When she kept motioning back toward the door, I would shake my head.

My aching dick had long since gone down when Mark walked up and joined the conversation.

Ari attempted to get up three times, but each time, Sue pulled her back down into a sitting position and told Ari that she never got to visit with her. I could see the sexual frustration building on Ari's face every time I looked over at her.

Then, the lights became brighter.

Mark looked at Sue and Ari and said, "The auction is starting."

I peeked over at Ari, and she was wringing her napkin.

Shit. If I didn't get her to the service hallway soon, we were both going to be in trouble.

Chapter Six

Ari

I **WAS GOING** to kill both of my parents. If they made it back to Texas in one piece, it would be a miracle.

I sat there and listened as the auction began. Jeff appeared to be enthralled in the bidding process, and he hardly even looked over at me. Each time he glanced over, I would try to motion to leave. Every once in a while, my mother would lean over and tell me to bid on an item. The last time she'd suggested I bid, I'd told her I was going to put her in the auction.

I peeked over at Jeff again. He looked so damn handsome in that tux. It was driving me crazy. I closed my eyes and imagined his hands on my body. I quickly opened my eyes and placed my hands on my flaming cheeks.

Jesus H. Christ. I need my husband, and I need him now. I'm kid-free! I want sex, damn it.

My mother motioned for me. "Oh, Arianna, a trip to France is coming up. You should bid, darling."

I snapped my head over to my mother. I opened my clutch and pulled out a tube of lipstick and a pack of gum.

I showed them to her and said, "Not happening, Mom. No money."

The bidding on the trip to France began. It included airfare, hotel, and something else I didn't catch.

"Come on, it will be fun. Just bid once," Mom said.

My mouth dropped open, and I glared at her. "In case you can't hear in your old age, Mom, the bidding started at five thousand dollars."

My mother swooshed her hand around like it was nothing. "One bid won't hurt."

I lifted my hand and imitated her hand movement. "Don't swoosh your hand around at me."

"Put your hand down, Ari," Mom said.

I snarled my lip. *How dare she treat me like a child.* I put my hand up and jerked it around again. "Swoosh, swoosh, swoosh!"

My father and Jeff turned and looked at me. Jeff had a look of horror on his face.

"Don't tell me I can't put my hand up in the air, and—"

"We have a bid of twenty thousand dollars by the beautiful lady in ivory. How about twenty-five thousand?"

I dropped my hand, and I was pretty sure I'd just pissed—sans panties—in my new gown.

"Oh, shit," I whispered.

Jeff's eyes grew bigger.

I mouthed, *Sorry*, to him as I smiled.

He mouthed back, *What the fuck?*

"We have twenty thousand going once..."

Holy hell.

"Twenty thousand going twice..."

Jesus, Mary, and Joseph, someone else bid!

Then, someone from behind me called out, "Thirty thousand!"

109

I instantly let out the breath I had been holding, and I looked at Jeff as he did the same thing. My mother and father started laughing.

"Damn it. I was really hoping you would have won that." Mom said.

I shot my mother a dirty look and stood up. "Excuse me. I need to check and make sure I didn't—"

"Ari..." my mother said as she glared at me.

"Jeff, I need to speak with you, please, in private."

My father began laughing again as he turned and faced Jeff. "I wish I had a camera, so I could have captured this moment and kept it forever. The look on your face was priceless."

I put my hand on my hip. "Daddy, stop being so mean."

I turned and began walking toward the back of the ballroom. I could feel Jeff right behind me. When he finally caught up, he put his hand around my waist and led me straight to the door. After one quick look back to make sure no one was looking, he opened the door, and we walked out. Jeff grabbed my hand and practically dragged me down the hallway. He made a right turn and then quickly turned around to face me. He pushed me against the wall and began lifting my dress as he dropped to his knees.

"Oh God, yes!"

I needed to come desperately. My body was so worked up from being pantyless all night, from Jeff looking hot as hell and touching me, and then from me almost spending twenty thousand dollars on a trip to France.

Jeff lifted my leg and held it up as he buried his face between my legs. He didn't even try to tease me. He went straight in for the kill. Within a minute, my moans were echoing in the halls as I had an intense orgasm.

My hands pulled on Jeff's hair as he kept going at it on my clit. My legs felt like they were about to give out when he put the leg he was holding over his shoulder, and he quickly unzipped his pants. He set my leg down and stood up as he pushed my dress up to my hips.

"Jeff, I want you so badly."

He smiled as he picked me up and guided his dick into me. I moaned in delight as he pushed himself deep inside me.

"Give it to me...please."

He held me against the wall and gave me what I so desperately needed.

"Does it feel good, baby?" Jeff whispered to me. He pulled out and then pushed back into me harder.

"Yes! Oh, yes! Don't stop. Jeff, I'm going to come again."

Jeff pulled out and slammed back in so hard that my head slammed against the wall while another orgasm hit me.

"Oh God," Jeff called out as he pumped in and out of me.

I could feel him pulsing inside me as he pressed his body against mine.

"Jesus, Ari. Being with you always feels like the first time," Jeff panted out.

I smiled when he slowly pulled out of me and set me down. He pulled a napkin out of his pants pocket and began cleaning me off. I leaned my head back against the wall as he gently took care of me. I never imagined I could keep falling deeper and deeper in love with him.

He stood up as he folded the napkin and then pushed it back into his pocket. He helped me smooth my dress back down, and then he zipped his pants.

He placed his hands on the side of my face and whispered, "I love you so much, Ari. Thank you for coming on this trip with me. I've missed being with you like this."

I nodded my head as I felt the tears building in my eyes, and I fought like hell to hold them back. We just stood there, staring into each other's eyes for the longest time. Our sex life was always good, but we hardly ever got to sneak away and just have spontaneous sex like this.

"What in the hell are you two doing?"

I smiled big as Jeff's eyes turned to horror. We both spun around and looked at my father.

"Trying to find a restroom," I said with a giggle.

My father narrowed his eyes at Jeff, and then he looked at me. "Follow me, Arianna. I'll show you where one is."

My father turned and walked around the corner as Jeff and I looked back at each other.

Jeff mouthed, *Holy shit. He's like Gramps!*

I busted out laughing and began walking out. I silently said a prayer, thanking God that my father hadn't come looking for us five minutes earlier.

Jeff and I danced almost the entire night. It was wonderful, magical, romantic, and beyond fun. I hadn't laughed so much in a long time. Jeff made a few new contacts, and we even made plans to check out another horse tomorrow.

When I smiled up at Jeff and raised my eyebrows, he laughed and shook his head.

"Baby, I'm exhausted. I think I'm getting too old for this kind of stuff."

I giggled. "My feet are killing me. Should we head back to the hotel since we are going to see that other horse tomorrow?"

He nodded his head and looked around. "Where did your parents go?"

I stopped dancing and glanced around the ballroom. "I don't know. Maybe they snuck off to have sex."

"Yuck. Gross. Man, I didn't need that image in my head, Ari."

I chortled as I grabbed his hand and walked back to the table. Jeff pulled out my chair, and slid it in for me and then took a seat next to me.

I leaned over and whispered, "As soon as we find them, I'll tell them we're leaving."

"So, Arianna, your mother tells me that you and your husband own a breeding business."

I smiled at the slutty-dressed woman sitting across from me. She couldn't have been much younger than me, and her breasts had been fighting with her dress all night.

"Yes, we do. We're also partners in Cattle Company as well."

Her eyebrows rose slightly as she looked over at Jeff. The way she eye-fucked him caused me to roll my eyes.

"Cattle as well? I've always wanted to see how a cattle ranch is run."

Jeff smiled politely. "It's just a bunch of cows grazing in fields most of the time."

She laughed, and her breasts began fighting to escape her tight dress. She began running her fingertips lightly across her chest, right above her cleavage.

What. A. Bitch. Hello? Wife is sitting right here.

Jeff reached for my hand and looked at me as he gently kissed the back of it. "Have I told you how beautiful you look tonight?"

I smiled because I knew what he was doing. "Yes, more than once."

He leaned over and kissed me tenderly on the cheek. "I love you," he whispered.

"I love you, too." I got lost in his green eyes.

"Arianna, do you work outside the home?" the bitch asked.

Without pulling my eyes from Jeff, I answered, "No. I help run the breeding business, and I train horses as well."

"Oh my. Do you have any children?"

I pulled my eyes from Jeff and looked over at her. *Why is she being so chatty and asking a million questions?* "Yes. We have a son, Luke, and a daughter, Grace."

Her smile faded a bit. "I see." She stood up and leaned down toward her date. She said something to him and then looked back at me. "Excuse me, won't you? It was a pleasure talking with you both." She looked at Jeff and winked. "Good luck with all those horses and cows."

He nodded his head and smiled. "Enjoy your evening."

I watched as she walked away.

My mother walked up and placed her hands on my shoulders. She leaned down to kiss me on the cheek. "Ari, dear, I'm exhausted. Your father and I are heading back to our hotel. Would you and Jeff like to have dinner with us tomorrow evening? We leave early the next morning."

I turned to her and smiled. "We're leaving then, too. Dinner with you and Daddy tomorrow would be great."

Jeff stood up and then reached for my hand to help me up. We followed my parents out of the ballroom and to the street.

My father looked at me and grinned. "If you don't want to your hotel yet, your car will take you anywhere y'all want to go."

"Thank you, Daddy, but Jeff and I are both exhausted. I think we are heading back to the hotel."

My father looked over at poor Jeff and glared at him.

I let out a giggle. "Daddy, stop being so mean to the love of my life."

He let out a gruff noise. "Dinner tomorrow evening around seven?"

"Sounds good, Daddy. Good night, Mom. Sleep well."

"Good night, sweetheart," my mother said. She kissed me on the cheek and then kissed Jeff.

My father reached out and shook Jeff's hand. "Good night, Jeff." He turned and gave me a hug as he whispered in my ear, "I see how much he loves you, and it warms my heat. But I will never let the little fucker know that."

He pulled away as I started laughing.

"Night, Daddy."

Jeff walked up and opened the door to our car, and I practically crawled inside. I was beyond tired. I just wanted to go back, take a hot shower, and go to sleep.

Jeff slid in next to me. "The Brown Hotel, please." He looked at me and asked, "What did your father whisper to you?"

I giggled. "He told me that he sees how much you love me, but he would, and I quote, 'never let the little fucker know that.'"

Jeff's mouth dropped open. "Why? Why does he like to torture me?"

I shrugged. "You'll probably do the same thing to some boy when Grace starts dating."

Jeff looked forward. "I won't have to because Grace will never date—ever."

I smiled as I snuggled up next to him, and then I began drifting off to sleep.

I felt Jeff lifting me as he took me out of the car. I lifted my head to see that he was carrying me into the hotel.

"Baby, I can walk," I said with a sleepy voice.

"Shh...I've got you."

I buried my face into his neck and took in his heavenly scent. He looked so handsome tonight, and as much as I wanted to make love to him again, I could hardly keep my eyes open.

Jeff somehow managed to open the door to our hotel room with me in his arms. He walked up to the bed and gently laid me on it. He gently removed my right high-heel shoe and began massaging my foot.

"Mmm...feels so good," I mumbled.

He repeated the process with my left foot. Then, he reached for my hands and pulled me up. He began unzipping my dress. He pushed the dress down some and then began kissing along my neck. He moved down to right above my breast.

He whispered, "Sit down and lie back, Ari."

As I lay back, I lifted my hips so that Jeff could pull my dress down. He quickly took the dress off of me, and he licked his lips as he took in my body. The only thing I was wearing now was an ivory lace push-up bra.

He ran his fingers along the bra and then down my cleavage as I closed my eyes. My whole body felt like it was on fire. He rolled me to the side just a bit, and after one of his movements, my breasts sprang free, and I let out a moan of relief.

He tossed the bra on top of my dress on the floor. He cupped both breasts and began massaging them. I could feel my whole body relaxing. My eyes grew heavier, and I tried like hell to focus on Jeff.

He gave me a crooked grin and whispered, "Go to sleep, baby."

I tried to respond, but all that came out was a, "Hmm..."

I closed my eyes and felt Jeff getting up from the bed. I could hear him taking his tux off, and then he made his way to the bathroom. I thought about how wonderful the last few days had been, and I still had two more days of nothing but Jeff, horses, passionate sex, and shopping.

What a lucky, lucky girl I am.

Then, I rolled over onto my stomach and let sleep take over.

Chapter Seven

Jeff

TODAY WAS OUR last day in Kentucky, and I was taking Ari everywhere she wanted to go. We had toured Churchill Downs and a few other historical places, and we were now getting ready to head out on the Belle of Louisville for a dinner cruise.

Ari turned to me and smiled. "It's our last night in Louisville, and this is such a wonderful way to spend it."

I wrapped my arms around her and kissed the top of her head. "It looks like the sunset is going to be beautiful. Are you cold?"

She shook her head as she turned and looked up at me. "You know, this trip was exactly what I needed. I feel so refreshed."

I grinned and nodded. "So do I. I miss the kids so much, but damn, five whole days without fighting kids or getting up at the crack of dawn to work has been like a dream. Plus, we've had hot sex more than once a day. We should stay another few days."

Ari hit me on the chest and winked. "As much as I would love to, I miss Luke and Grace something terrible."

"I do, too, baby. I do, too." I kissed the tip of her nose.

We stood in silence as the steamboat headed out.

During dinner, we sat next to a couple who were also from Texas. They would be moving from Texas to Kentucky, and they were visiting to buy land here. We had a blast with them.

The sun began to slowly fade away, and the colors dancing on the river were beautiful as Ari and I stood on the deck of the boat.

I was suddenly overcome with sadness. "I miss Luke and Grace."

Ari looked at me, and her eyes were filled with sadness. "I do, too. I can't stop thinking about them. Grace hasn't texted me all day. Ellie took her and Alex shopping in Austin today. What if Grace wants to stay there when we get back?"

I threw my head back and laughed. "Ari, please. I'm sure she has just been so busy having fun, and that is the only reason she hasn't sent us a text. Besides, it's Ellie. She can't stand shopping."

Ari chewed on her bottom lip. "What about Luke? I haven't heard from him today either."

"He had a baseball game today. Gunner texted earlier and said they were winning."

"See? If they'd won, Luke would have texted us by now. Our children have moved on without us!"

I laughed and pulled her into my arms. "No, they haven't."

She frowned. "Have you heard from Luke at all today?"

I had sent Luke a text earlier. I'd wished him good luck at his game, but I hadn't received a reply. I hadn't thought about it until just now. "Um...now that you mention it, no, I haven't heard back from either one."

"See? Oh my God. Your sister has stolen the love of our kids. That little bitch!"

I started thinking. "Come to think of it, I texted good night to both of them last evening, and I never heard from them."

Ari let out a gasp and threw her hands up to her mouth. "Me either." She dropped her hands as she began looking around frantically.

"What are you looking for?"

"A way off the boat. I need to get back to my kids!"

"What? We leave tomorrow morning, and there is no way off the boat. Are you insane?"

She spun around and poked me in the chest. "This is all your fault. I said to let your dad and Carol watch them. But did you listen to me? No. You said to let them stay with Ellie and Gunner. They'd have fun, you said. Well, look at what we've got now."

I shook my head and tried not to laugh. "Ari, you seriously think our children wouldn't want to come back home?"

She nodded her head quickly. "They've forgotten us."

I had to admit it. My heart was beginning to hurt a little from just thinking about Luke not texting me to tell me about the game.

I grabbed Ari and pulled her back into my arms. We both stared out and watched the sunset.

When my cell phone dinged with a text message notification, I practically pushed Ari away from me. I pulled my phone out and saw a text from Luke.

"Aha! He texted me! He sent me a text. Pesh...see!" I shoved my phone in Ari's face.

She frowned and pulled out her cell phone. "Nothing," she whispered. She looked back at me and tried to smile. "What did he say?"

I opened up his message and read it aloud.

> **Luke: Hey, Dad! Hope you and Mom are having fun. Sorry I didn't text last night or earlier today. Uncle Gunner took Colt and me hunting last night and this morning. It was fun, but it wasn't as fun as when you and I go. We won our game! Kiss Mom for me, Dad. I miss you both. I'll be glad when y'all come home tomorrow. Oh...by the way, I kind of hit Will. He said he liked Alex. Uncle Josh wasn't too happy with either one of us. I kind of have a black eye from fighting with Will.**

I looked up at Ari and smiled as I saw a tear rolling down her face. I quickly blinked my eyes to keep myself from tearing up.

Damn, I love that boy.

Ari began laughing. "He *kind of* has a black eye?"

I shook my head. "He is so protective over Alex. I think he will be more protective than Colt will be."

Ari wiped away her tear. "I miss them."

Then, her phone went off. She began jumping up and down. "It's from Grace! It's from Grace!"

"Read it to me!"

Ari smiled. "Hey, Mama, please tell me you are still coming home tomorrow. Oh my gosh, Aunt Ellie took us to the mall. Mom, it was awful. Did you know she hates shopping? Who hates shopping? I miss your good-night stories, Mama, and Daddy's good-night hugs. I can't wait to see y'all."

Ari started crying as she dropped her arms to her sides and looked at me. "They still love us!"

I let out a chuckle and pulled her into a hug. "I told you, baby. I told you."

Ari's knee was bouncing a mile a minute as we drove to the airport. "He's gonna make us miss our plane," she hissed through her teeth.

"We have plenty of time, Ari. Stop worrying."

She let out a sigh. "Um...are we close to the airport, sir?"

Right after she asked, the cab driver turned the corner, and right in front of us was the airport.

I grabbed her hand and kissed it. "We'll be home in a few hours, baby."

She smiled weakly. "I just want to see the kids."

"I know. Me, too. Grace will be happy that we have three new horses heading our way."

Ari chuckled. "Yeah, she will."

After getting our luggage out of the taxi we headed into the airport and checked in our luggage before making our way to the gate.

It didn't take long before we were sitting in our seats, and the plane was taking off for Austin. Ari fell asleep, and she slept during the whole flight while I worked on my computer. Every now and then, I would look over at my sleeping beauty and smile. I silently said a prayer and thanked God for the blessings in my life.

Ari must have been exhausted because she was still asleep when the plane landed.

I gently nudged her shoulder and kissed her cheek. "Baby, we landed."

She sprang up and quickly took off her seat belt. "It's about time. What a long flight!"

I looked at her like she was insane. "How would you know? You slept the whole time."

She rolled her eyes and pushed me out into the aisle. I reached up into the overhead bin, pulled out her carry-on, and handed it to her. I was pretty sure she was about to push the older couple in front of us out of the way if they didn't speed it up.

After exiting the plane, I laughed as I tried to keep up with her as she practically ran to baggage claim.

She turned and said, "You get the truck. I'll get the luggage and meet you out front."

I kissed her on the cheek. "Yes, ma'am. Text the kids and let them know that we will be there in a couple of hours."

She clapped her hands and did a little hop.

I made my way to the truck and then headed to the pick-up curb in front of the baggage claim doors. Ari was already standing there, talking on the phone to someone. I couldn't help but smile as I saw the huge grin on her face.

She must be talking to the kids.

I jumped out of the truck and grabbed the suitcases. I put them in the bed of the truck as Ari went on and on about how proud she was of Luke. My heart soared when she told me that Luke had hit two home runs.

I held the door open for my beautiful bride as she hopped up into the truck. I ran around and got into the driver's seat. Then, we headed off toward Mason. The closer we got, the more excited Ari and I got.

"Next time, I say two days. I think two days is about all I can take being away from the kids."

"I agree. Gunner told me that he has already made arrangements to take Ellie to a bed-and-breakfast in Fredericksburg. I say we follow their lead next time we want to get away."

Ari snapped her head toward me and let out a gasp. "Yes! Oh my gosh, what a great idea. We would be away but not really too far away. Brad and Amanda have been doing something like that for a few years now. They go away for a weekend each month. Usually, their parents take the kids for the weekend, and Amanda and Brad lock themselves in the house and fuck like rabbits. Why the rest of us never thought of doing the same thing is beyond me."

I let out a laugh and nodded my head. "Well, from now on, I'll make sure we get some *us* time."

Ari and I talked about Sweet Dancer most of the way home. Layton Morris had called back, and we made arrangements to have Dancer sent straight to his ranch for his trainer, Lucky, to start working with our new horse. In exchange for the training, Layton wanted to breed a mare with Charmer. It was a win-win situation for both of us.

Ari began jumping around in her seat as I pulled up to the gate. I thought she was going to jump out and push the gate open.

"Oh my God. Has our gate always opened so damn slow?" she asked.

I started down the driveway, and when we pulled around to the barn, our kids were there with my dad and Carol.

Ari's hands went to her mouth, and she began crying. "They look bigger!"

I laughed and put the truck in park as Ari threw the door open. She jumped out and ran toward the kids.

"Mommy!" Grace yelled. She ran and jumped into Ari's arms.

Luke stopped just short of Ari, letting her hug and say hello to Grace. I couldn't be more proud of my son. He was so much like me that it was unreal, but he also had Ari's caring heart. Ari set Grace down and then held her arms open for Luke. He walked straight into her arms and held on to her as he told her how much he had missed her.

I quickly wiped away the tear from the corner of my eye before the kids turned their attention to me.

Grace's face lit up when I smiled at her. "Daddy! Daddy!"

I bent down, and she slammed her body so hard into me that I almost fell backward.

"I missed you so much. Please tell me we are getting new horses!" she said.

I laughed and hugged her tightly before letting go. "How does three new horses sound?"

She let out a scream and began jumping up and down. I glanced up and saw my son waiting patiently for his turn.

I kissed Grace on the cheek and whispered, "Your mama bought you some new clothes."

Grace's mouth dropped open, and then she did a little fist pump before running back to Ari. "Mama, show me my new clothes!"

Ari laughed as she nodded her head, and then she walked toward the truck. I looked back at Luke as he came up to me and put his hand out for me to shake it.

"Dad, I'm really glad y'all are home."

I shook his hand and then pulled him into a hug. "Me, too, son. Me, too. While the girls go crazy over clothes, how about I take the suitcases into the house, and you go help

Bandpa saddle us up a couple of horses? Then, we can go for a ride."

He nodded his head quickly. "I'd love that!"

I glanced up and saw my dad smiling as Luke took off running to the barn. I walked up, shook my father's hand, and kissed Carol on the cheek.

"Thanks y'all for bringing them home for us."

My father smiled as he watched Luke. "That boy is so much like you it's unreal. You're going to have your hands full with him, son."

I turned and watched as Luke jumped and tried to hit the top of the barn door. He was nowhere near close to it, but I gave him props for trying.

"You're telling me, Dad."

I took the suitcases into the house, and Carol, Ari, and Grace all made their way to our bedroom to see the outfits Ari had bought for Grace. I rolled my eyes when Grace began gushing over the clothes. She was, for sure, a mini Ari.

I made my way down to the barn, and as I walked up, I could hear my father and Luke talking. I stopped and stood there for a few seconds, taking it all in. Growing up I had missed these moments with my father, but I was thankful that he was here and able to be such a huge part of my life as well as Ellie's and our kids' lives.

"Bandpa, are you riding with us?"

"I figured you'd like to spend some time with your dad since you haven't seen him for a few days."

"I'd like to spend time with both of y'all," Luke said.

My heart soared. Whatever Ari and I were doing with our kids, we were somehow doing it right. I took a deep breath in and tried to contain my crazy emotions as I walked into the barn. When I saw the smile on my son's face as he looked at me, my whole world stopped, and I took this moment in.

Moments like this just brought me back to the day when I'd known my life would never be the same. It was the day I'd sat under an oak tree, and the love of my life had saved me.

The End

Faithful

BOOK THREE IN THE WANTED SERIES
SHORT STORY

Chapter One

Heather

JOSH AND I made our way up the stairs, stepping oh-so quietly. Will and Libby had been sleeping for over two hours, and I had been in pure heaven. The house had been so quiet that we just sat on the sofa and took it in while we massaged each other's shoulders, backs, and feet. Then, Josh had gotten the idea of heading upstairs for some much-needed *us* time. I was a bit pissed that we had wasted over two hours sitting on the sofa before one of us thought of it.

We walked into our bedroom, and Josh turned on the upstairs monitor.

I quickly stripped out of my clothes and jumped into bed. Josh quickly began undressing.

"Fast. We have to go fast. They've been asleep for far too long," I said.

Josh nodded his head and began kissing my breasts. He moved his lips up my neck, and I let out a soft moan. When I felt him pushing against me, I spread my legs open wider. The moment I felt his heat inside me I about came.

"Josh," I whispered.

I gently moved my fingertips up and down his back as he slowly and passionately made love to me.

"Heaven," Josh said as he pushed in deeper.

"Yes."

Then, we heard something. We both instantly stopped moving and snapped our heads over to the monitor.

"Oh God, Will is up!" I said as I watched Will sitting up in his bed.

One quick glance at Libby's bed showed that she was still sleeping.

Josh and I quickly looked back at each other.

"Move! Josh, go!"

Josh began moving in and out faster. As much as I wanted him to take it slow, I knew we had a limited amount of time now that Will was up. Soon, he would start calling out Libby's name to wake her up.

"Harder!"

"Jesus, Heather. Faster, harder—I'm trying, damn it. I just wanted to enjoy you."

I shook my head. "I know, I know! God, it feels good. I'm sorry, baby, but hurry."

Josh grabbed my hips and began moving faster and harder.

With each thrust, he said, "They. Can. Wait. A. Few. Minutes."

"Oh God, Josh, I'm so close."

"Heather, I'm going to come."

"No, wait!"

And just like that, it was over.

As soon as Josh collapsed on top of me, Will started calling out, "Libby! Libby!"

I closed my eyes and wanted to cry. I hadn't had an orgasm the last three times we had sex. I was long overdue for one. I opened my eyes, and I watched Josh jump up from the bed, and he started getting dressed.

I got up on my elbows and frowned at him. "What happened to letting them wait for a few minutes? I need relief, too."

Josh gave me that crooked smile of his, and I fell back onto the bed and pouted. He walked up to the edge of the bed and opened the drawer in the side table.

He reached in for the vibrator. "Is this what you want?"

I jutted out my bottom lip and shook my head. "I wanted to come with you inside me."

"Wibby! Wibby, get up!"

I looked at Will jumping up and down in his bed.

Turning back to Josh, I smiled. "That'll do. Hurry! The little monster knows how to open the bedroom door."

Josh quickly began moving the vibrator in and out. He sat down next to me, and the moment he put his mouth on my nipple, I lost it. I didn't mean to call out so loudly when my orgasm hit me, but I did.

Will must have heard me because my orgasm was cut short when he yelled, "Mommy! Mommy!"

I opened my eyes and looked at Josh, who was attempting to hold back his laughter.

"Baby, I promise to take care of you tonight."

I pushed his hands away and got up. I quickly got dressed and began stomping out of the bedroom. I turned and looked at him. "Three. I want three orgasms tonight."

Josh's eyes lit up, and he nodded his head. "You got it, baby. Three it is."

I smiled as I turned and headed downstairs. When I opened the door to the twins' room, Will was sitting on Libby's bed, holding her hand. My heart melted. Libby had Will wrapped around her little finger. He was fiercely protective of her, and he had already gotten into a scrape with Luke when he pushed her.

I smiled as Will looked at me and grinned. He held his fingers up to his mouth as if he was trying to tell me to be quiet.

"Wibby is sweeping, Mommy."

I nodded my head and stuck out my hand. He jumped down from his bed and walked toward me. Getting to spend one-on-one time with just one of the twins would be a rare treat.

As I was heading out the door with Will, he stopped, turned, and let out the loudest scream I'd ever heard.

"Wibby! Wake up!"

My mouth dropped open, and Libby immediately sat up and began crying. Josh walked past me and quickly scooped her up into his arms. He couldn't stand to hear her cry or know she was scared.

I couldn't help but grin as she instantly stopped crying the moment Josh had picked her up.

I barely heard her say, "Daddy."

Josh walked around with her for a few seconds while I changed Will.

I glanced back at Josh and said, "Do we try again?"

Josh let out a sigh and nodded his head as he set Libby down. "Come on, y'all. Let's try to go potty."

Libby went screaming down the hallway. Will started to drop his drawers in the hallway, and he was about to pee on the wall.

"No, Will!" Josh and I both yelled out, scaring him.

The second I saw the lip pout, I knew we were done for.

Josh and I quickly dropped down on the floor and began trying to make him giggle.

That was when I heard a crash.

"Mommy..." Libby said in a hushed voice.

I fell back onto my butt and let out a long sigh as I dropped my head into my hands.

Josh stood up and headed toward the living room. "We will survive this, Princess. We will survive."

Chapter Two

Josh

I PACED BACK and forth as I waited for my mother to answer her cell.

"Hello?"

"Mom!"

"The desperation in your voice almost makes me want to giggle. It brings back a memory of you in your crib, taking off your diaper."

I rolled my eyes. "Really, Mom? You have to bring this up again?"

"You clean poop off a wall and tell me you wouldn't bring it up every chance you got."

"I was, like, three, Mom!"

She let out a loud laugh. "I know. Oh, man, sweet revenge, and I didn't even have to lift a finger."

"Mother, this is serious. I need to get Heather out of this house. I will totally pay for a nanny to come in and help you for a couple of days." I pushed my hand through my hair, and when I felt something slimy and wet, I quickly jerked it to the front of my face. "Applesauce?"

"What? What about applesauce? I was saying, your father and I would love to come and stay for a few days. We don't need a dang nanny to take care of our own grandchildren."

I placed my hand back in my hair and let out a gasp. "How did they get so much applesauce in there?"

"Oh Lord, I'm packing a bag right now."

She hung up the phone before I could even say anything else.

I was about to hit Gunner's name on my phone when a text came through.

Mom: My friend Nancy can come and help your father and me out if needed. Don't worry. Take Heather somewhere and spend some time together.

I loved my mother more than anything right now. I pushed Gunner's number and glanced back toward the house.

"What's up?"

"Gunner, I *need* your help!"

"I truly thank God every day that I didn't have twins."

"Ha-ha. I need to get Heather out of the house, but I need to stay close to home."

"I'm on it. There's a bed-and-breakfast place right outside of Fredericksburg. I took Ellie there once. How many days?"

I instantly thought of Heather saying she wanted three orgasms. "Three nights. If Heather wants to come back earlier, we can."

"I'll call you back with the details."

"Text me. I need to take a quick shower and get applesauce out of my hair."

Gunner started laughing, and then he kept laughing, so I hung up on his ass and jogged into the house. Heather was standing at the kitchen island. She was talking to Will and Libby as they ate Goldfish pretzels.

She looked at me and smiled. "Will here wants to give it another go on the potty."

I smiled and shook my head. "No way, little man. It's almost bedtime."

Will made a face while Libby gave me that look that melted my heart and made me want to give her anything she asked for.

Not tonight, little one.

I looked at Heather and smiled. "Princess, I need you to pack us a bag with enough stuff for three days."

Her smile faded, and her body slumped. "Josh, it's so hard to travel with them."

I looked down at the two little devils as they glanced back and forth between Heather and me. I leaned down and kissed them each on the head. Then, I turned back to Heather. "It's just you and me."

"What? Oh God, if you're kidding with me right now, I'm totally cutting your ass off for two weeks!"

I laughed. "Let me jump in the shower and get the applesauce out of my hair. Then, I'll help with getting them ready for bed."

Heather let out a little scream and jumped into my arms, which only led Libby to scream in excitement. Will used the moment to take his bowl of Goldfish and toss it across the island.

"We so need this," Heather said, holding on to me tightly.

"God, I know. Um...baby, you need a shower, too. You have applesauce in your hair."

I pulled up and parked outside the Magnolia House Bed and Breakfast, and Heather let out a sigh.

"Oh my gosh, it is so darling." She spun around and smiled. "Let's go!"

I jumped out of my truck and jogged around to the other side where I opened Heather's door. She had packed a small suitcase for us, so I grabbed it from the backseat and then took her hand in mine.

After we walked in, we were greeted by Lisa, the owner of the bed-and-breakfast. "Josh and Heather, it's such a pleasure to meet you both."

Heather extended her hand. "Thank you so much for having us."

Lisa smiled. "Where are y'all from?"

"Fredericksburg," I said before thinking.

Lisa's smile faded for a quick second before returning. "Oh. Well..."

"We have three-year-old twins," I added.

Lisa nodded her head. "Oh, honey. This is your retreat for the next three days. I'm at your service for whatever you need."

Heather and I both let out a small chuckle.

"I've been told your breakfast is the most amazing thing we will ever eat," I said.

Lisa's face lit up. "Why, yes, it is. You'll find out tomorrow morning."

Heather peeked at me through her eyelashes. I was pretty sure we were both thinking the same thing. There was no way in hell I would be getting up in time for breakfast tomorrow.

"Let me show you to your room. Now, your friend booked the Magnolia Suite. That is our most romantic room. You have a private entrance, so you can come and go as you see fit."

When Lisa opened the door Heather let out a soft gasp.

"It's beautiful. Look at the antique furniture. Oh my goodness, the mural is beautiful. It almost looks like we are in Italy!" Heather said.

I smiled as I set the bag down on the sofa. There was a small sitting area near the fireplace. I walked out onto the patio and smiled. This was just what Heather had needed—complete relaxation. I was planning on spoiling the hell out of her while we were here.

I walked over and glanced into the bathroom. It was small but looked like it had been updated recently. When I stepped back out, Heather was walking Lisa to the door—or rather, Heather was practically pushing Lisa out the door.

"I think it would be safe to say that we probably won't be joining y'all for breakfast tomorrow. I'm going to want to sleep in." I said with a smile.

Lisa smiled sweetly as she nodded her head. "Of course. I completely understand. Enjoy your evening."

"Thank you, and thanks again for letting us check-in so late," Heather said before shutting the door.

She turned and leaned against the door as she gave me the sexiest smile. When I smiled back, she began frantically stripping off her clothes, and I did the same.

"Josh, I just want to make love—slow, sweet, and passionate love."

I walked over, picked her up, and carried her over to the bed. I gently laid her down and then moved next to her. She rolled onto her side and placed her hand on my face.

"I love you, Josh Hayes. I love you more and more every day."

"I love you, too, Princess. I feel the same way. I didn't think I could ever love you more, but each day, I swear, my heart falls more in love with you."

She closed her eyes and whispered, "Make love to me, Josh."

I moved over her and slowly pushed into her warm body and completely lost myself in her.

Chapter Three

Heather

I SLOWLY OPENED my eyes and took in the room. I was wrapped in Josh's arms, and I had never felt so relaxed. I smiled as my mind drifted back to last night.

"Heather," Josh whispered against my neck as he slowly moved in and out of my body.

My hands were pinned above my head with one of his hands as the pressure in my body began to build. I arched my back as he rubbed the one spot that would take me to heaven and back.

"Josh...I'm going to come."

As he pushed deeper into me, I softly began to call out his name between my moans of pleasure.

"Oh God, Heather, I'm coming."

His hot breath against my neck was one of my favorite things. Josh slowly pulled out of me, and then he pulled me close to his body.

He softly said, "You're my everything."

I grinned. "And you're mine."

"Baby, are you up?" Josh whispered.

I turned around until I was facing him. "Yep. I have been for a few minutes. Just taking in the feeling of not having to jump up and run to the twins."

"I thought maybe we could walk around town. Then, we'll have a nice, relaxing lunch before coming back here and having pre-dessert."

I giggled. "Pre-dessert?"

"Yeah, dessert is like a treat. I want to save my treat for later tonight."

I raised my eyebrow at him. "What do you have in mind for dessert?"

He slowly sucked in a breath of air and let it out. "A little bit of whipped cream, maybe a few cherries, and some chocolate syrup. I want to make my own personal sundae."

"Hmm...that sounds yummy."

"Yes, it does."

"I think that sounds like an amazing day. I'm going to take a shower first."

Josh nodded his head. "Me, too."

I pushed him back and laughed. I got up and made my way to the bathroom and pushed the curtain back and turned the faucet to warm. I ran my hand through the water until it was the perfect temperature. I stepped into the shower and let the water run over my body. It felt so good, knowing I wasn't going to have to jump in, quickly soap up, and then jump out to dry off and get dressed.

When Josh entered the shower, I turned and grinned as he flashed that beautiful smile of his back at me. My heart began pounding when I saw him reaching for the removable showerhead. Josh adjusted the setting on the showerhead to massage.

Oh God.

"Turn around, Princess, and put your left foot on the edge of the tub."

I quickly did as he'd asked. He pushed my back some to get me to arch it. When I felt him pushing against my entrance, I let out a moan. Then, I felt the warm water on my clit, and I jerked as Josh pushed inside me. It wasn't going to take long at this rate. Between the heat of the water and the friction of Josh moving in and out of me, I was going to come fast.

He moved the water closer to me, and that was it.

I placed my hand on the shower wall in front of me and began calling out his name. "Josh...oh God...yes!"

I called out Josh's name over and over as one of the most intense orgasms gripped my body. Josh dropped the showerhead and grabbed on to my hips before he began moving faster and harder.

"Ah...Heather...I'm coming."

Josh and I came down from our orgasms as we stood in the shower, panting. He leaned down and picked up the showerhead. Then, he used his foot to inch the leg I was standing on farther out while my other foot was still on the tub. Josh began running the warm water between my legs, and it felt like heaven. I'd thought I was relaxed before, but I was even more relaxed now. I closed my eyes and took in the feeling of the warm water running over my sensitive body. After Josh put the showerhead back up, he touched me, and my body reacted with goose bumps.

"I love making you call out my name," Josh said as he took me into his arms.

I chortled. "I love when you make me call out your name."

"Want to go shopping?"

I pulled back and shook my head. "I want to go looking for land."

The smile that spread across Josh's face caused me to giggle.

We had been tossing around the idea of moving out Fredericksburg for the last couple of years. The only thing holding us back was the fact that Josh's parents had moved to Fredericksburg to be closer to us. Josh had talked to them about it the other night, and they had both encouraged him to do it. Gunner and Jeff needed help, and more than anything, Josh wanted to be out there, working next to his two best friends.

"Baby, have I told you lately how much I love you?"

I nodded my head. "You have. Just remember this when it comes time to design the house."

"God, I want a big house, Heather. I can't deal with our little house anymore."

Josh turned and shut off the water before reaching for a towel. I stayed in the shower and dried off as he stepped out and quickly did the same. Then, he wrapped the towel around his waist and made his way out of the bathroom. I licked my lips as I watched his perfectly toned body walking away from me.

How in the world did I get so lucky with him?

After getting dressed, I sat down on the sofa while Josh looked up some properties. He pulled out his cell phone and called the real-estate agent we had talked to the other day.

"Patty, hey, it's Josh Hayes. I'm doing well. Listen, Heather and I are kid-free today, and we would love to go look at land in Mason. Are you free?" Josh turned and looked at me. He grinned from ear to ear. "Perfect. We'll be there in ten minutes."

I tried to calm the butterflies in my stomach. I wanted to move to Mason and be closer to Ellie and Ari, but the idea of leaving the first home I'd ever bought made me nervous. I thought of all the memories made in that house—our children being born there and all the times Josh and I had made love. I jumped when I felt Josh's hand on the small of my back.

"I know what you're thinking. We'll make new memories."

I slowly nodded my head as Josh led me out the door and to his truck.

An hour later, we were pulling up to a ranch that was one hundred acres. It was just down from the Mathews' cattle ranch.

"Wow. We're just down the road from Ellie, Ari, and Jessie!" I jumped out of the truck and followed Josh over to where Patty was standing.

"What do y'all think?" Patty asked.

I looked out over the beautiful Texas hill country. It was breathtaking.

"If this was my place, I think I'd want the house right here for an almost three-sixty view of the whole ranch," Patty said with a huge grin.

Josh and I looked at each other.

Could this really be it? It's the first place we've looked at.

I had the most overwhelming feeling of peace come over me. Seeing this place first was almost like it was meant to be.

"It just came on the market this morning. Y'all are the first to look at it."

The smile that spread across Josh's face made me chuckle.

"A sign?" Josh asked.

"I'd say."

He tilted his head and narrowed his eyes at me.

I nodded my head and said, "Yes."

Josh quickly turned around and faced Patty. "Let's put an offer down on it."

Patty's sweet smile faded. "Huh?"

"An offer, Patty. Full price. I don't want to miss out on it."

"Oh, um...well, um...y'all don't want to look at any of the other listings?"

Josh shook his head. "Nope. This is it."

"Okay. Well, let me call the seller's agent and let her know that a full-price offer is fixing to come through."

Josh clapped his hands together and did a little jump. When he turned back to face me, I ran into his arms and wrapped my legs around him, and then he spun us around. When he stopped, I looked into his eyes and knew he felt it, too.

"Welcome home, Princess."

It was almost as if my father had spoken through Josh. I didn't even attempt to hold back my tears. In this moment, I knew what was happening was meant to be. We were going to start our new life here on this hilltop.

Patty laughed. "All right, kids, let me call the selling agent, and then we will head back to the office."

"Okay, Patty." Josh set me down and placed his hands on my face. "I feel it. Do you feel it?"

I slowly nodded my head and bit down on my lower lip to keep from crying harder.

"Our kids are going to grow up in the most beautiful place. They'll have so much room to run around."

I tried to speak, but I couldn't. I looked out over to the west. We would have the most amazing views of the sunset. I closed my eyes, and I could picture myself sitting on a porch swing, watching Libby and Will playing. When I opened my eyes, I saw something moving. I focused on a buck walking across the open field. He stopped and looked at me as I stared at him.

I turned to Josh. "Josh, look at the buck." I glanced back and pointed, and then I dropped my hand.

He was gone. I quickly scanned the area for him.

"What buck, babe?"

I slowly shook my head. "He was...right there. Didn't you see him? He was huge."

"Nope, I didn't see him at all. I'm sure we will see a ton of deer out here. I can't wait for the kids to see all the wildlife."

I smiled slightly as I looked around. Josh began talking about building a tree house and where we could put a pool in if we ever wanted one. I laughed as he began planning everything out. I peeked back over to where I had thought I saw the buck, and there he was again, standing in the same exact spot as before. I smiled as he turned away from me and began walking into the tree line.

Yes, this is definitely home.

Chapter Four

Josh

HEATHER AND I sat down at our table at the Rose Hill restaurant. I didn't think either one of us had stopped smiling since we signed the offer on the land in Mason.

"I still can't believe the seller accepted the offer so fast," she said.

I smiled and nodded my head. "I know. What do you think about having Jeff or Gunner design the house?"

"I think that's a wonderful idea!"

The waitress walked up, smiled at Heather, and then turned her whole body toward me. "Good evening. Welcome to Rose Hill. May I start you out with a glass of wine?"

"I'll just take a Coors Light if you have it." I glanced over to Heather.

She said, "I'll have the same."

The waitress never once stopped smiling at me. "Are you here celebrating anything special?"

She moved her eyes up and down me and then stared straight at my lips. I quickly looked away and smiled at Heather, who grinned warmly back at me. I leaned forward and reached for her hand.

With my hand on top of hers, I said, "Yes. My beautiful wife and I are celebrating how very much in love we are."

Heather shook her head slightly as she narrowed her eyes at me and grinned.

The waitress took a step back. "Wonderful. I'll bring your drinks as well as two glasses of water over shortly."

"Thank you so much," Heather said as she continued to look into my eyes.

When the waitress walked away, I sat back.

"I can't take you a restaurant without waitresses flirting with you, can I?"

I let out a laugh as I watched Heather lean back in her chair.

"Have you heard from your mom yet?"

I pulled out my cell phone and checked it. "Nope. You want to text her, or should I?"

"Nah. I'll send her a quick text."

Heather typed out a message to my mother as the waitress returned with two beers and two glasses of water. We placed our dinner order, and then we immediately began talking about ideas for the house.

"It has to be a two-story home, but this time, we'll be on the first floor, and the kids will be on the second."

"I completely agree," I said. I smiled when an older waitress set my salad down in front of me.

"I'm also thinking we should have a game room for the kids to play in upstairs." Heather let out a small squeal. "Oh my gosh, just think, we can twin-proof this bitch good!"

I laughed and took a bite of my salad. "How many bedrooms? I'll need an office for sure."

Heather smiled. "Four bedrooms, one being for guests. Oh, Josh, you can finally build the shop you desperately need."

"I know. I was already thinking where I want to build it. We could build a barn and have the shop somehow attached to it. We could maybe even put an office down there as well."

"That would be perfect."

The rest of the evening, we discussed the house and made plans to talk to Jeff and Gunner about the design.

By the time we got back to our room at the inn, we were both mentally exhausted. After we walked into the room, Heather collapsed down onto the bed.

"I feel like my brain has worked overtime tonight," she said.

I let out a laugh and lay down next to her. "I hear ya. I don't want to talk about houses, barns, and shops anymore."

Heather rolled over and began running her finger in circles on my chest. "You still owe me three orgasms."

I turned my head and looked into her eyes. "What kind of husband would I be if I didn't deliver those to you?"

She ran her tongue along her lower lip and shrugged her shoulder. I sat up and pushed Heather onto her back. I moved my eyes up and down her beautiful body. I reached over and began lifting her skirt, and my stomach dropped as I thought about burying myself deep inside her. When my fingers brushed against her bare lips, I raised my eyebrow up at her.

"Jesus, have you not had panties on all night?"

She giggled. "No."

"Why didn't you tell me?" I quickly moved between her legs and pushed them open. "Hmm...shit...that looks good." I let out a moan. I began kissing her inner thigh, and then I moved my lips closer to heaven.

I blew on her clit, and she bucked her hips.

"Josh, don't tease."

I let out a chuckle as she grabbed my head and pushed me closer to her. The moment my tongue touched her, she let out a moan. It didn't take her long to start moving her hips as she called out my name.

When I finally didn't feel her pulsing anymore, I pulled away and quickly began getting undressed. Heather sat up and pulled off her skirt. Then, she began unbuttoning her shirt, and she tossed it onto the floor. I reached behind her, and in one movement, I had her bra unclasped. I took it off and threw it next to her shirt on the floor.

My eyes traveled up and down her body as I licked my lips in anticipation.

"Jesus, Heather, you're so damn beautiful. I can never get enough of you."

She wrapped her legs around me, and I slowly sank into her warmth and began slowly making love to her.

"You feel like heaven." I closed my eyes and took in the moment.

Heather always brought all my emotions to the surface when we made love like this. There was nothing I loved more than being with her. We were one...for always.

My lips moved across her neck as she made the sweetest noises. My body craved her touch. I wrapped my arms around her and brought her closer to me. I needed more of her.

"Josh..." she whispered.

I softly kissed along her jawline. When my lips landed on hers, she sucked in a breath of air. I wasn't sure how long we had been kissing, but when I pulled away, I pushed harder inside her. I must have hit the perfect spot because Heather let out a gasp, and I could feel her squeezing down on my dick.

I leaned my forehead against hers. "Princess, I'm going to come."

"Josh...I love you."

The love and tenderness in her voice caused my heart to skip a few beats. The moment was so beautiful, and I didn't want it to end.

"I love you," she said again, her voice cracking this time.

I wiped away a tear moving slowly down her cheek. I stayed inside her as our bodies began coming down from our orgasms.

"I love you forever...plus infinity, Heather."

Chapter Five

Heather

I COULDN'T HELP but let out a giggle as I read Elizabeth's text message.

> **Elizabeth: I don't know how you keep up with these two!**
>
> **Me: I don't know either, believe me!**
>
> **Elizabeth: Did you know that Will can open the bedroom door?**
>
> **Me: Yep. He figured that one out a few weeks ago.**
>
> **Elizabeth: Don't worry, honey. We are about to head to the park. Everything is going great!**
>
> **Me: Thank you so much for doing this!**
>
> **Elizabeth: We love these little sweethearts.**

Josh came walking out of the room, laughing, and he sat down next to me on the private balcony.

I glanced up and smiled. "What's so funny?"

"Dad said Will had a bowl of oatmeal and tossed it across the kitchen. Mom tried to run and catch it, and he said it was probably the funniest thing he had ever seen. He said she actually dived for the bowl."

"Oh my gosh. Did she get hurt? I was just texting with her. She didn't mention it."

Josh began laughing harder. "Dad said she did a complete split, but I'll be damned if she didn't catch the bowl!"

I threw my hands up to mouth and began laughing. "Oh. My. God."

"I know. Hell, I would have paid top dollar to see that show."

"Joshua Michael Hayes, that is not nice!"

Josh kept laughing as I giggled and pictured my poor mother-in-law doing a split across our kitchen floor. He finally got his laughing under control, and then he mumbled something about paybacks.

"I'm totally loving just the quiet," I said.

He reached for my hand and gently kissed the back of it. "I'm glad, baby. You deserved some quiet time."

We sat there in silence, and I closed my eyes and took in all the sounds.

"Heather, have you thought any more about that teaching position?"

My heart dropped, and I opened my eyes. Mason Elementary had offered me a teaching position, and I had turned it down. When the principal had told me I could have a few days to think it over and change my mind, that was all I had been doing, except for the last two days. It hadn't even entered my thoughts until now.

"Not really. As much as I would love to go back to work, I just don't think I can, Josh. I can't leave Will and Libby."

I glanced over at him, and he was smiling.

155

He almost seemed relieved. "That's your final decision?"

I nodded my head and said, "I love being home with the kids and you. I can help with the business and take advantage of nap time." I wiggled my eyebrows up and down.

Josh laughed. He stood up and reached for my hand. I gave it to him, and he pulled me out of my seat.

He brought me into his arms. "You have no idea how happy I am to hear you say all of that. I will always support you in whatever you want to do. Having you and the kids home though is what I really want."

I grinned and reached up to kiss his lips. "Do you know what I really want?"

He angled his head and gave me a sly look. "What do you really want, Mrs. Hayes?"

"To be thoroughly fucked by my husband."

"Your wish is my command, Princess."

He pulled me through the door and into the room before dropping my hand. I stood there and watched my husband as he stripped out of his clothes, and my sex began to pulse. I would never get used to this incredible need to be touched by him and to feel him slowly take over my body and make it his.

He walked over to his bag and opened it. When he pulled out handcuffs, my stomach clenched, and I could feel my panties getting soaked.

"It's playtime," he said.

I pulled my shirt up and over my head and shimmied out of my pants. Josh walked up to me and began running his finger along the top of my breasts. I let out a small moan as he slowly licked his lips and captured my eyes with his. He reached down, and in one quick movement, he ripped off my panties as I sucked in a breath of air. I loved when he did that. It turned me on even more—if that were possible.

"Get on the bed, Heather. You know what to do, baby."

I had never moved so fast in my life as I did when getting onto that bed. I lifted my hands above my head and smiled as Josh handcuffed them to the antique metal frame. He leaned down and began kissing along my neck from one side to the other before moving down to the edge of my bra.

"Oh God," I whispered.

"I'm going to fuck you hard but not fast. I want to take my time enjoying you."

My mouth dropped open, and I tried to talk, but nothing came out, except for a faint moan. My body was aching for him.

"I need to feel you inside me," I whispered.

Josh grinned as he placed soft kisses all over my body. Each time a kiss landed on my sensitive body, I could feel the wetness growing between my legs. When his lips touched the inside of my upper thigh, I about jumped off the bed.

"Josh! Yes! Oh God, yes. Please don't make me beg."

He chuckled. I was too worked up to do anything but will him to move his lips to my clit. He slowly pushed his fingers inside me.

I hissed out, "Yes!"

"Heather, you're so wet. Do you want me?"

I thrashed my head back and forth. I needed to touch him. I needed him to touch me. I needed to come.

"Fuck...Josh...please."

"Trust me, baby. I will fuck you good and hard, but I want to play first."

He began running his tongue up and down my inner thigh.

Jesus...

I was going to come without him even touching me where I needed him most. I could feel the build up growing stronger and stronger.

"Yes. Oh God, yes!" *This one was going to be big.* I jerked on the cuffs and let out a frustrated moan.

Josh slipped his fingers inside me. "Damn, I can't wait to bury myself deep inside you."

I pushed my hips up and whined. "Now. Josh, do it now!"

He smiled and slowly got up. He grabbed my legs and pulled me up and off the bed. My breathing began to grow faster and heavier as he inched closer. I could feel his tip teasing my entrance.

"Oh God..." I was going to come the moment he pushed into me, and I couldn't wait.

"Hold on, Princess. I'm about to—"

Then, there was a knock on the door. Josh and I stopped moving and stayed perfectly still.

"Josh? Heather? I brought y'all lunch."

Josh's mouth dropped open in shock as we heard Mindy, our neighbor, on the other side of the door. I shook my head quickly and wanted to cry.

I shot Josh a dirty look and mouthed, *Are you kidding me?*

He dropped my legs and jumped off the bed. "I forgot that Dad said he told Mindy where we are staying when she asked where we were."

He started getting dressed as I lay cuffed to the bed. I had never been so mad in my entire life.

What in the hell is that bitch doing here? And why in the hell is he getting dressed?

"What are you doing?" I whispered.

He looked at me like I was crazy. "Getting dressed!"

"Why?" I asked through clenched teeth.

He stopped and looked at me funny.

All those insecurities came flooding back. *Does he want to see her? He waves to her every time he runs by her house. Does she still have a thing for him? Is he attracted to her?*

She knocked again. "Josh? Heather?"

He looked at the door and then at me.

"Get me out of these," I said as I jerked on the cuffs.

He quickly walked over and unclasped my hands. I got up and pushed him out of the way. I reached for my robe and stormed off to the bathroom. I leaned against the door as I heard Josh answer the door.

"Hey there, Mindy! Sorry. I was sitting outside, and Heather is in the shower."

"My, my, Josh. You must be working out."

Her voice grew louder, so I knew she must have walked into the room. I could practically feel the steam coming from my ears.

"Let me grab a shirt."

My mouth dropped open. *He opened the door without a shirt on?*

I looked around the bathroom and found a pair of my jeans and a T-shirt. I slipped them both on and then threw my hair up into a ponytail. I opened the bathroom door quickly.

Mindy jumped. "Oh my! Heather, you gave me a fright."

I just glared at her. I slowly turned my head and glared at Josh.

"Your father told me you two were taking a break for a few days, so I thought I would make you a home-cooked lunch for today. You could enjoy it out on the patio."

"That was really kind of you, Mindy," Josh said.

I snapped my head over and stared at him. My heart dropped, and I wanted to cry.

Who brings lunch over to a hotel, for Christ's sake?

I glanced back at Mindy. I barely smiled at her as I walked over and slipped on my flip-flops. Josh gave me a questioning look as he watched me.

I grabbed my purse and looked at Mindy. "I'm sorry for being rude, Mindy, but you interrupted us with your little lunch delivery. It appears my husband thought it was more important to answer the door and have lunch with you than to fuck his wife, so I hope you both enjoy your nice home-cooked meal." I turned my attention to Josh. "Try not to choke on it, Josh."

Josh stood there, stunned, as I pushed past him and headed out the door. I pulled the door shut behind me so hard that it slammed and rocked the paintings hanging on the walls. I quickly wiped the tears away as I walked through the dining area and living room. Once I hit outside, I began running—or rather, I tried to run the best I could in flip-flops.

I knew I was acting like a child, but something had snapped inside me, and I began to have all those feelings from years ago again. I just needed some time to get myself pulled together. I turned to see if Josh was coming after me, and when I didn't see him, I cried harder.

I finally came to a stop and leaned against a building. I put my head in my hands and continued crying as I slid down the wall. I sat there on the ground, crying and acting like a child, as I tried to figure out why my heart felt like it had just been ripped out.

Chapter Six

Josh

I WASN'T SURE what I was more shocked by—the fact that I had been about to have sex with my wife, and I'd stopped to answer the fucking door, that Heather had just said what she said and walked out the door, or that Mindy had had the nerve to come here.

"Josh, are you and Heather having trouble? Is this little stay here to rekindle something lost?"

I glanced up at Mindy. She was moving her tongue along the top edge of her teeth.

Fuck. I should have known things would never change with this girl.

I walked up to her and grabbed her arm. She let out a gasp as I pulled her to me.

"Yes, Josh, yes," she said as she smiled.

"I thought you understood where I stand with you. I am *not* interested in you, and I never will be. I love my wife, and right now, I'd love to kick your ass for interrupting what we were about to do."

Her smile dropped. I reached for the basket of food and guided her to the door. I opened it, pushed her out the door, and handed her the basket.

"If you'll excuse me, I need to find my wife." I slammed the door shut in Mindy's face.

I quickly ran over and put my sneakers on. I grabbed my cell phone and went out the side door before jogging to my truck. I got in and hit Heather's number. It went to voice mail.

"Heather! Baby, please, don't do this to me, Heather. I'm in my truck, and I'm going to drive around this town all fucking day if I have to."

I hit End and started the truck. I slammed my hands down on the steering wheel, and then I ran them down my face.

Why didn't I just ignore the fact that Mindy was at the door? Why?

I was about to put the truck in reverse when someone knocked on my window. I turned to see Heather standing there with tears streaming down her face. I threw my truck into park, turned off the ignition, and opened my door. I jumped out, slammed my door shut, and pulled Heather into my arms.

"I'm. So. Sorry," Heather cried out.

I began running my hand down the back of her head. "Shh...Princess, please don't cry."

She cried harder. "I don't know what...came...over me."

I reached down, picked her up, and carried her back to our suite.

"No, Heather, it's me who should be sorry for doing what I did. Baby, please forgive me. I wasn't thinking. I just kind of panicked that she was there."

I slowly put Heather down when we were inside our room.

She wrapped her arms around my neck. "I love you, and I trust you. I'm so sorry I acted like that. All those...the bad feelings...it all just—"

I slammed my lips to hers and started kissing her passionately. She moaned as I slipped my tongue in, and I moved her closer to my body. She pushed her hands through my hair, and I pulled her hips to mine, so she could feel how much I wanted her.

She pulled her lips from mine and whispered, "Josh..."

I quickly pulled her shirt over her head and began taking her jeans off as she fumbled with my jeans. We both pushed our pants down and kicked them off to the side. She hadn't put panties on, so I grabbed her and picked her up. She wrapped her legs around me as I turned and walked up to the sofa. I set her down on the back of it.

I wiped the tears away as I looked into her eyes. "You are the only woman I have ever loved and will ever love. It's always been you, Heather. It will always be you."

I pulled her to me and slammed my dick inside her, and she let out a gasp. I moved in and out of her, fast and hard. It was as if I was afraid that she would tell me to stop at any moment. I had to make her mine again.

"You're my whole life."

"Yes..." She panted. "Harder."

"You're mine, Heather."

I grabbed her hips and moved faster.

"God, yes...yours...Josh...I'm gonna come. Oh God, yes! Yes!"

I could feel her pulsing down on me, and it was my undoing. I came so hard that I let out a moan and called out her name over and over. I hadn't had an orgasm like that in a while. I pulled her to me and picked her up as I continued to pour myself into her.

She wrapped her arms around me and held on to me so tightly. "I love you, Josh. I love you so much."

I walked us into the bathroom. I didn't want to pull out of her, but I slowly did, and I gently put her down. I turned and started the shower. I stepped in and then reached my hand out for hers.

I picked up the soap and began cleaning her whole body off. She dropped her head back and made the sweetest noises as I took care of her. I washed every single inch of her beautiful body and then quickly washed mine as she rinsed off.

We made our way to the bed and crawled under the covers. I pulled her body up against mine as we lay there in silence. Nothing needed to be said. I could feel the love pouring from her body, and I hoped like hell she could feel mine.

I slowly began to let my body relax.

"I love you, Josh."

"I love you more."

"I love you more...plus infinity."

I smiled as I drifted off to sleep. I dreamed of our new house with Will and Libby running in an open field, laughing, as a massive buck stood guard, watching them.

Three Months Later

"Will! Stop pulling Alex's hair!" I shouted.

Alex went running to Ellie.

Heather was attempting to chase down Libby, who was running and screaming because a fly was after her.

"Okay, we need another plan of action. These four kids are going to drive me to drink!" Ellie said.

Jack and Grace started laughing.

Grace put her fingers to her mouth and whistled loudly. "Who wants watermelon?" she called out.

Jack walked up to Gunner's truck and put the tailgate down. Then, he pulled out a cooler.

Will, Libby, Colt, and Alex all ran up to them. With Colt being the youngest, he'd learned quickly that he had to be fast, or he would miss out, and he was the first one there. Grace picked him up, handed him a huge piece of watermelon, and set him down in the bed of the truck. Soon, all four of them were sitting down there, eating.

I let out a sigh as I pulled Heather into my arms, and then I kissed her.

She smiled and looked over to Gunner. "I love your mom and dad."

Gunner laughed. "So do I. So. Do. I." He picked up the plans again. "So, if you think you're happy with the layout of the house, the only other thing to do is decide where you want the house to be placed."

Heather walked up and pointed to the plans. "Those wraparound porches are going to be heaven. I'd love to have the house face north and south but maybe slightly turned, so the back porches face the west a bit more. The sunsets out here are amazing."

Gunner nodded his head. "I totally agree with you, Heather. The idea is to take advantage of the views. The ceiling-to-floor windows across the back wall will make it feel like y'all are outside, even when you're inside."

"I think that is my favorite thing so far." Heather said with a smile.

"I love the row of window seats you are putting in the dining room," Ellie said.

I glanced over to Heather. She was gazing down at the plans with the biggest smile on her face.

"So, when are they gonna start building?" I asked.

Gunner began rolling up the plans. "Monday."

My heart soared. We were building our dream home—a place where our kids would grow up, a place where we would make all new memories.

"Gunner, thank you so much for recommending the builder who built your place," Heather said. She leaned up and gave Gunner a peck on the cheek.

"It's my pleasure. They built Jeff and Ari's main barn as well, and Jeff was really pleased. I think you will be surprised when you see how fast the builder can get things going."

I glanced back toward the kids. Right at that moment, Will took a handful of watermelon and smashed it into Colt's face as Libby distracted Jack and Grace. Colt screamed, Alex started crying—I had no clue why—and Libby and Will high-fived each other.

"When did Libby and Will learn how to high-five?" I asked no one in particular.

Gunner and I began walking toward our kids.

He laughed. "Damn, dude. You have your work cut out for you."

I nodded my head and whispered, "Tell me about it."

Chapter Seven

Heather

SITTING AT THE kitchen table, I jerked my head up after it bobbed when I began falling asleep.

I had just put Will and Libby down for their afternoon nap. They had been sleeping with us for the last four nights. They were cuddlers, so there was no sleeping for either Josh or me when they were in bed with us.

Josh had come up with a great idea though. We'd pushed their beds together and made one big bed. When I'd put them down for a nap, they'd both snuggled up next to each other. I'd smiled as I watched them drift off to sleep. They really were thick as thieves.

Josh walked into the kitchen and stopped when he saw me. "You look like how I feel."

"Thanks," I said, sliding my chair back. I walked to the refrigerator and opened it. "Is it too early to have a drink?"

He let out a chuckle as he walked up behind me and reached in for the sweet tea. "How about a tall glass of tea?"

I let out a sigh. "Sure."

"How long have they been asleep?"

"Maybe an hour."

A sexy smile spread across his face as he glanced down at the island and raised his eyebrow. "It's been a while."

I was just about to unbutton my pants when we heard laughing. We both stopped moving and stood perfectly still.

Libby started laughing again.

"Is she dreaming?" I whispered.

Josh made a face. "I don't know."

"Will! Will! Will!" Libby chanted.

I put my hand over my mouth. "She's gonna wake up Will!"

Josh looked over at the monitor and began laughing. I spun around and let out a gasp. Will was jumping up and down on the bed while Libby clapped her hands and chanted his name.

"You made them a trampoline in their room!"

"Look at Libby egging him on!" Josh laughed.

I slowly turned and glared at him. I wanted him to feel my anger.

He peeked down at me and said, "What?" He pointed to the monitor. "You have to admit, that is some funny shit right there."

I placed my hands on my hips. "So, now that they can jump on their beds like a trampoline, where do you think they'll want to sleep tonight?"

Josh's smile faded. "Fuck. I didn't think about that."

I quickly turned, walked out of the kitchen, and made my way to the twins' room. After three more weeks, the house would be done, and we would be moving in. Then, Will and Libby would have their own rooms. I opened the door, and Will continued to jump.

"Hey, Mommy!" he shouted.

Libby sprang up and began jumping, too. I closed my eyes and counted to ten. I opened them and placed my hands on my hips. Will and Libby both stopped jumping. Libby sat down while Will just stood there.

"You both know better."

"Mommy, are you mad?" Libby asked in the sweetest voice.

My heart wanted to melt, but I refused to let it.

"Yes, Mommy is mad. Both of you, off the beds. We do not play or jump on the furniture at all."

They both jumped off as I made my way over to Will's bed. Josh walked into the room just then, and he helped me push Will's bed back against the wall. I turned and looked down at the twins. Will was resting his chin on his hands, and Libby was twirling her hair with her finger.

"God, look at how cute they are," Josh whispered.

Ice. Cold as ice. "In a few weeks, the two of you will be in your own rooms."

Will stood up and did a little fist pump as Libby started crying. Will dropped to his knees and began trying to comfort her.

Oh. My. Goodness. He is just like his father. My heart Flipped my stomach.

I looked over at Josh as he smiled and watched our son comforting our daughter.

I glanced back at them. *My sweet little angels.*

No, Heather. Must. Remain. Cold. As. Ice.

I took in a deep breath and slowly let it out. "Libby, you're a big girl now. You and Will get to have your own rooms. Just think of all the extra room you'll have."

"For toys?" Will asked with a smile.

Josh chuckled.

I hit him in the stomach. "Don't encourage him."

"Sorry."

"Maybe—if you are a good little boy and girl. That means, no jumping on beds, no putting mud in Mommy's shoes, no bringing frogs inside and putting them to bed in Libby's bed—"

Libby began giggling, which I found funny since she'd screamed bloody murder when she found said frogs in her bed.

Will nodded his head. "Okay, Mommy."

I smiled as I bent down and wiped away Libby's tears. "Don't cry, baby girl. You're going to love your new bedroom."

She stood up and stepped into my arms. I picked her up and held on to her.

Josh held Will's hand. "Come on, buddy. Let's go potty."

Josh took Will upstairs while I led Libby to the bathroom downstairs. Weeks ago, we'd figured out that we needed to separate them to potty-train them faster. It had only taken days until they were both one hundred percent potty-trained. We wouldn't even have to put Pull-Ups on them during naps. We would just use them at night, and most nights, they would both wake up dry.

We were halfway through dinner, and Libby had already successfully put spaghetti up her nose and in her hair. Will had spent more time constructing something out of his spaghetti than he had eating it.

"What are ya making, buddy?" Josh asked.

I kicked him under the table. "We don't play with our food, Daddy...remember?"

Josh smiled at me and then turned to Will. "Hey, buddy, let's start eating, okay? We'll build something with your blocks before bedtime."

Will's face lit up. He quickly grabbed handfuls of food and pushed it into his mouth.

"Slow down, William."

Will gave me a smile and slowed down.

Dinner continued without any more problems, and I silently thanked God for the peaceful meal. Afterward, Josh took Will and Libby and gave them a bath while I cleaned up.

Later, we were all sitting in the living room, playing, when my cell started ringing.

I jumped up and ran to answer it. "Hello?"

"Hey, Heather."

"What's up, Jessie?"

"You and Josh feel like having a night off?"

My stomach did a little flip at the idea of being alone with Josh. "Are you playing a cruel joke on me? Or are you offering something up?"

She laughed. "No joke. Scott has a huge benefit dinner and dance to go to in Austin, and I don't want to be stuck there alone with no one to talk to. I arranged for a friend of mine from college, who is now a full-time nanny, to come and stay here for the night. Do you think Josh's parents would take care of your kids? We are staying in Austin the whole night."

I bit down on my lower lip and glanced out into the living room. A whole night alone with Josh would be amazing.

"I have to ask Elizabeth. I think she's still recovering from the last three days they watched the twins."

"It's a ball. We can dress up and feel beautiful."

I scrunched up my nose. I really wanted to go. "Damn it. When is it?"

She let out a little yelp. "This Saturday night."

I took in a deep breath and quickly blew it out. "Let me call Elizabeth. I'll call you right back."

Josh walked up to me and kissed me on the cheek. "What's going on? Why are you calling my mom?"

"Jessie said Scott is going to this huge benefit dinner and ball in Austin on Saturday night. They want us to go. We'd have to stay in Austin all night though."

Josh's eyes lit up instantly. "All night?"

I chewed on my bottom lip as I nodded my head.

He took my cell phone from my hands and began calling his mother. "Hey, Mom. No, it's me. How are you and Dad? Oh, yeah?"

I peeked in the living room, and Will and Libby were busy constructing something.

"That's awesome, Mom. Hey, not to cut right to the chase 'cause you know I love hearing about how you and Dad are doing in the garden. Yes, I was being facetious, Mom."

Josh winked at me and motioned for me to follow him. We walked out into the living room and both sat down next to the kids. Libby handed me a block, and when I placed it on top of hers, she clapped.

"Heather and I have been invited to a dinner and ball in Austin on Saturday night. I'd love to be able to take Heather." Josh smiled and gave me a thumbs-up. "Mom, you're the best. We owe you and Dad big time. Right. Yes, I'll tell her. Hold on. Lib and Will, y'all want to say hi to Grammy?"

Libby's eyes lit up as she jumped up quickly and then sat in Josh's lap. "Gammy! Gammy, I wuv you!"

Josh smiled and nodded his head as he pointed to Libby talking to Elizabeth on the phone. "If Mom had said no, I was gonna pull out the big guns."

I covered my mouth and laughed.

Will and Libby each talked to Elizabeth and Greg for a few minutes.

"Okay, Mom. I'll give you more details as I get them. I love you, too."

Josh hit End, and we high-fived each other.

I called Jessie back, and as soon as she answered, I said, "We're in!"

"Perfect! It's at the W Austin Hotel. Dinner starts at six, and the ball immediately follows it. I guess we'll just meet y'all there?"

"Sounds like a plan."

"See you then, sweets!"

I hung up and ran upstairs.

"Where are you going?" Josh called out.

I stopped and turned back to look at Josh. "I need to see if I have a dress. If not, I'm going shopping tomorrow."

Libby jumped up and ran toward me. "I want to dwess up, too, Mommy!"

I reached down for her and picked her up. We made our way upstairs and into the master bedroom. I set Libby down in my closet, and I began looking at my dresses.

I smiled when I saw the white dress bag. "Oh, Libby! Mommy has the perfect dress!"

Libby clapped her hands. Then, she began putting on my shoes, and she attempted to walk around in them. I hung the dress up on the hook and unzipped the bag.

When I saw the red chiffon backless dress, I smiled. I had bought it a few months ago when Ari, Ellie, Jessie, and I had gone shopping in Austin. Ari thought a girl could never have too many sexy evening gowns, and she was right.

Josh was going to die when he saw me in this number.

I looked down at Libby and said, "Daddy is going to love this. The high slit comes all the way up to the top of my thigh."

I jumped up and down, causing Libby to do the same.

She reached for the dress and said, "Me!"

"No, not this one, baby girl."

I turned and grabbed a white sweater. I slipped it over her head, and she wobbled to the mirror in my high-heel shoes.

She looked in the mirror. "Oh...so pwetty!"

I laughed. "Yes, you are." I zipped the dress bag back up and walked over to Libby. "Want to show, Daddy?"

She smiled big and nodded her head. I picked her up and took the shoes off her feet. I carried them as we made our way downstairs. Josh was in the twins' bedroom, getting Will ready for bed. When we walked into the room, I slipped the shoes on Libby's feet and then set her down.

Josh's face dropped at first, and then he smiled big. It made us both sad to see the kids growing up so fast.

"My goodness. You look like a princess in that beautiful dress and those shoes. My heart might never recover from seeing such a beautiful young lady."

Libby blushed and began rocking back and forth. "Tank you," she said.

She looked up at me, and I grinned.

"Okay, Princess, time for bed. Lift those arms up, so we can take your beautiful dress off, and let Mommy take the shoes back upstairs." I said as I helped Libby take off the sweater.

Josh and I each snuggled up with the kids, and he read them a quick story. Will passed out as soon as Josh had begun reading the story. We tucked them in and kissed them good night. Libby had a new thing where we had to touch her hand three times before we could leave and shut the door.

After that, I slowly closed the door and looked up at Josh. "Say a prayer that they stay in their own beds tonight. I need sleep."

He tapped my nose with his finger and said, "Not until I have my wicked way with you."

My stomach clenched, and I grabbed his hand as we quickly made our way to the stairs.

"Mommy..."

I let out a small, "No..."

I slowly turned around to see Libby standing in the hallway with her bear.

"Pwease lie down with me. Pwease..."

I kissed Josh on the lips and said, "I'll be up as soon as she falls asleep."

He nodded and headed upstairs. I took Libby's hand and walked her back to her bed. I tucked her in and lay down next to her.

"Night, baby doll," I whispered.

She snuggled up next to me. I listened for a few minutes until her breathing became slower. I started sneaking out of the bed when Libby grabbed my arm. I closed my eyes and gently lay back down.

This went on for at least an hour. Every time I moved, she would wake up.

I lay perfectly still until I was sure she was sound asleep. When she finally drifted off to sleep, I carefully slid out of the bed and onto the floor. I moved softly and quietly across their bedroom floor. Just as I made my way to the door, it opened. I held my breath in fear that it would wake up Libby. I looked up from my position to see Josh staring down at me.

He mouthed, *What are you doing?*

I motioned for him to back up and leave the room as I crawled out. I got on my knees and slowly shut the bedroom door. When I turned away from the door, Josh had his pants down, and his dick hit me in the face.

He grinned and said, "While you're down there..."

Chapter Eight

Josh

I WAS PRETTY sure Heather was going to be pissed because I'd just shoved my dick in her face. She looked up at me like she wanted to say something, but then she did the one thing I hadn't expected.

She took me into her mouth.

I placed my hand on the wall as she moved her mouth slowly up and down my dick.

"Oh God..." I whispered.

Heather hated blow jobs with a passion. She looked up at me and hummed, and I about lost it. I tapped her on the shoulders, and she sucked hard one last time before letting me go.

She stood up and wiped the side of her mouth. "Wow, I must be getting good if you were about to come that fast."

I shook my head. "It's called not expecting it."

She smiled and began walking toward the steps. She up a few steps and stopped. She slowly pushed her shorts down and then hooked her fingers under her panties. She sat down on the wooden stairs and moved to the edge. When she spread her legs open, I let out a moan.

"My turn," she softly said.

I dropped to my knees and quickly buried my face between her legs.

"Oh...yes..."

We usually never did anything like this out in the open since the twins started opening their bedroom door, but tonight, something had come over both of us. Her hands began pulling on my hair as she pushed my face in closer to her. I slipped two fingers inside her, and she let out a gasp.

"Oh yes...Josh," she whispered.

I flicked my tongue faster against her clit as I pushed my fingers in and out. I began sucking on her clit, and she lost it.

"Oh God...shit...shit...shit..."

I looked up as she had both hands covering her mouth, and her eyes were closed. I loved making her come. I quickly began kissing up her body, and then I slipped inside her and slowly started moving in and out. I was about to come, so I pulled out and lifted her up.

I carried her into the kitchen and set her down on the island. "Lie down, Heather."

She moved and lay down. I crawled on top of her, and I pushed inside her warmth. I couldn't believe how wet she was.

"Jesus, you're always so ready for more, Heather."

"Yes. Hard, Josh. I just want it hard."

I began giving her what she wanted. Each time, I would slam into her a bit harder, and she would let out moan after soft moan.

"Fucking yeah," I hissed between my teeth.

She lifted her shirt and bra and started playing with her breasts. I grabbed on to her hips and pulled her up some as I began pumping faster and harder.

"Yes! Yes! Oh God, yes! Ah..."

I could feel her squeezing on my dick, and I was just about to come when I heard, "Daddy? You're not supposed to jump on the furniture."

My dick instantly went down. I stopped moving and looked at Libby standing there, clutching her teddy bear in her arms.

"Motherfucker," I whispered.

I glanced down at Heather. She was laughing so hard that she had tears running down her face.

Somehow, between her laughing and crying, she managed to say, "Finally! I'm not the one deprived of an orgasm!"

I quickly pulled out of her and reached in a drawer for a hand towel. "Very funny, Heather."

I got down as Heather pulled her bra and shirt down.

She looked at me and said, "My pants are, um..."

Then, Libby turned and walked away. I began following her as she made her way back into her bedroom, and then she climbed up into bed.

Oh dear God, we have a sleepwalker.

I couldn't believe my eyes when Heather stepped out of the bathroom. She was wearing a beautiful red dress, and she grinned from ear to ear as she spun around.

Oh, holy hell.

The damn dress was completely open in the back, and the slit damn near came all the way up her leg.

"I really want to have sex with you right now."

She busted out laughing and shook her head. Her beautiful blonde hair was pulled up, and she had simple diamond stud earrings on. She walked up to me and placed her lips right next to my ear. The smell of her perfume filled my senses, and for a brief moment, my knees felt weak.

"I'm planning on more than just sex, Mr. Hayes. I want to be fucked six ways from Sunday."

I swallowed hard as she blew into my ear. My dick instantly came to attention. She took a step back and moved the dress open, so I could see the red lace crotchless panties.

"Mother of all things good." I snapped my eyes up to her. "Are you trying to kill me?"

She bit down on her lower lip and slowly shook her head. She grabbed her clutch purse and slipped on her red high-heel shoes. "Let's go." She turned and walked out.

I stood there for a few minutes, trying to regain my composure. I heard Heather talking to my parents downstairs as I tried to get my rock-hard dick to go down.

I needed to be inside her...and soon.

"Josh, is everything okay? You've been distracted all through dinner," Scott said.

I pushed my hand through my hair and shook my head. "My wife is slowly trying to drive me mad."

Scott let out a chuckle. "Can't be as bad as what Jessie did to me before we walked into the hotel."

I peeked over at Jessie. She was listening to an older man talking to her and Heather about banking. They both looked bored out of their minds.

"What did she do?" I asked, turning back to Scott.

"She told me she had those damn balls inside her, the ones Ari had bought them all. Look at her damn face. It's all flush. She's fucking killing me."

I let out a laugh. "Damn."

"What about you?"

"Heather is wearing crotchless panties, and she whispered something to me before we left the house. I can't remember what she said exactly. All I heard was, *I want to be fucked.*"

Scott had been taking a drink of water, and he spit it out as he started laughing and choking at the same time. Jessie and Heather both looked at him. Heather glanced over to me with a questioning look, and I shrugged my shoulders.

"Are you okay, honey?" Jessie asked.

Scott held up his hand and said, "Fine. Sorry. Went down the wrong way."

I laughed as I patted him on the back. "When is this damn thing over? I'm ready to head up to the room."

Scott looked around. "I don't see why we couldn't sneak out now. Maybe one more dance with my girl to get her worked up again, and then we're fucking out of here."

I stood up quickly. My dick was so hard that I was ready to take Heather right here on the damn table. "Sounds good. I'll talk to you later, dude, if we don't see you before we leave."

Scott laughed and whispered, "Horny bastard." He walked past me and asked Jessie to dance.

I couldn't help but notice that Jessie instantly blushed. I was going to have to ask Heather about those balls.

I leaned down and whispered against Heather's ear, "Dance with me?"

Heather placed her hand in mine and stood up. I led her out to the dance floor and pulled her toward my body, closer than I probably should have. Her eyes filled with passion, and she quickly looked around.

Leaning in, she placed her lips next to my ear. "I'm ready to leave."

"Okay." I grabbed her hand and started toward the exit. She began chortling as I practically pulled her along.

"Wait. What about Scott and Jessie? We didn't say good-bye."

"Trust me. Scott's not gonna care."

I walked us to the elevator, and we stood next to an older couple. I glanced over and smiled at them as they smiled at me.

"You look beautiful, my dear...just like a princess," the gentleman said to Heather.

Heather's head snapped over, and she looked at him.

The lady chuckled. "You do look lovely, darling. Enjoy this evening out. I know it can be hard when you're away from your children. The key to a happy family is a happy husband and wife."

"What did you say?" Heather whispered as her body began to shake.

I took a step closer to her. She was holding her breath like she always did when she got nervous or scared.

"Breathe, Princess, breathe," I said.

She sucked in a shaky breath, and a small sob escaped her mouth.

The lady tilted her head. "I'm so sorry. I didn't mean to upset you."

Heather shook her head and attempted to smile. "No, it's okay. It's just that...my mother used to say that all the time, and...well...my parents passed away during my senior year of high school."

They both smiled warmly at Heather. "My dear, I'm so sorry, but you have to know your parents never really left you. They've been here, watching over you, the whole time."

Heather wiped a tear away and nodded her head. "Yes, I know. I feel them often."

I glanced down and noticed the man was holding a baseball cap in his hand. It had a buck on it. I quickly looked at Heather to see if she had seen the hat. The elevator door opened, and we all stepped inside.

I moved our key card in front of the pad and pushed the top floor. "Which floor?"

The gentleman said, "We're going all the way up, son."

I smiled and nodded my head. "The suites here are amazing, aren't they?" I asked.

He grinned back at me from ear to ear. "I've been in a far better one, that is for sure."

As the doors shut, the lady took Heather's hand in hers. "Now, I can read people very well. From you, my dear, I can tell you are a wonderful mother. Stop being so hard on yourself. There is no manual to tell you how to raise your kids. Your children know you love them. And by the way your husband gazes at you so lovingly, I can tell that you are very loved by him. Let him take care of you and love you."

Heather looked stunned. She slowly nodded her head.

The elevator doors opened, and the couple stepped off.

The gentleman turned and looked at us as we stepped out of the elevator. "Smile big and love even bigger."

Heather and I both let out a chuckle.

"Thank you," Heather said.

The couple said good-bye and began walking down the hallway, holding hands.

But I noticed the gentleman wasn't carrying his baseball cap anymore. I quickly looked into the elevator before the doors shut, and I scanned the floor. "Where did the baseball cap go, the one he was holding?"

Heather looked at me. "He wasn't holding a baseball cap."

I looked back at them before they turned the corner. "Yes, he was. I wanted to point it out to you because it had a buck on it."

Heather slowly shook her head. "No, he didn't because—"

She stopped talking and looked back down the hallway. Her mouth dropped open slightly as a tear rolled down her face.

"Earlier this evening, when we were driving in, I kept thinking about my parents. I wished my mother were here, so I could ask her questions about Libby and Will. I know I have your mom, but I wish I could get some advice from my own mother."

I felt the tears building in my eyes.

Heather smiled and whispered, "My parents. I know that makes me sound crazy, Josh."

I looked back down the hallway. I took off running to catch up with the couple. I turned the corner, but no one was there. I turned and ran back to Heather. I took her by the hand, and we made our way to our room.

Once inside, I picked up the phone and called the front desk. There were only four suites on this floor, so it should be easy to find out which one the couple was staying in.

"Hi, um...this is going to sound weird, but we rode up in the elevator with an older couple, probably in their mid- to late sixties. He dropped something in the elevator, and I'd like to return it to him. Do you know which room they're in?"

"I'm sorry, Mr. Hayes. It is only you, Mr. Reynolds, and a young woman staying in the suites. There is no older couple."

I sat down on the bed. "Okay...thank you." I hung up and looked at Heather.

She was smiling the most peaceful smile I'd ever seen on her face. "My parents."

I slowly nodded my head. "Your parents."

Chapter Nine

Heather

LAST NIGHT HAD probably been the most amazing night of my life. I smiled as I touched my lips and thought of Josh softly whispering against them, telling me how much he loved me. I thought of the couple on the elevator and how I'd had the most overwhelming sense of peace wash over my body after she talked to me.

Josh and I had made love three times throughout the night. The first time had been the most beautiful. It had been slow, passionate, and full of nothing but pure love. The second had been in the bathtub. Josh had taken his time giving my body such careful attention. The third had been early this morning when I woke up to him tying me up and then blindfolding me. It had been hot and passionate love-making, the kind where I could totally just let myself be free.

I smiled and shook my head as I looked out over the breathtaking garden. I took in a cleansing, deep breath. I would miss this house, but I knew what we were doing would be better for us and for the kids. We would make beautiful, sweet memories in the new house.

"Mommy! Mommy, I'm up!"

I stood and headed back into the house. I opened the door to the twins' room and smiled when I saw two beautiful faces looking back at me. Libby began clapping, and she jumped out of bed following Will. He always stopped and let Libby hug first. It warmed my heart that he was already so kind and generous at his age. When Libby pulled back, Will showed his true three-year-old boy side. He pushed her to the side and bear-hugged me.

"Will, you do not push your sister. Apologize now, please."

Will looked down at the ground. "I'm sowwy."

Libby smiled and kissed Will on the cheek. Life was good again—until they both ran to the bathroom and began fighting over who would pee first.

I closed my eyes and thought, *Just a few more weeks.*

I flopped down onto the sofa and let out a long, drawn-out moan. We had been unpacking for hours in the new house and I was exhausted.

"Good Lord, we have a lot of shit."

I laughed and agreed with Josh. "Yes, and most of it is the kids' stuff."

"Did you see Libby's face when she walked into her room?"

I nodded my head and giggled. "I don't think she had any idea that when she'd said pink and green, that was what she was getting."

Josh chuckled. "When she saw the butterflies that Ari had painted on the wall, I almost shed a tear from how excited she was."

"What about Will and his horse-themed room?"

"I'm telling you, Ari could make another career out of painting murals. Did you know she could paint like that?"

I giggled. "Yeah. With Matthew having Fragile X, he is a visual learner. Ari began taking art classes when she was really young. She used to draw things for Matt. She actually taught Matt how to paint."

"Jeff told me that Matt was asked to be in an art show in Austin."

"Yep. He is so excited about it."

Josh yawned as he glanced over to me and pushed my leg. When I looked into his eyes, they were filled with nothing but lust.

"I want to take you on every surface of this house."

I felt my stomach clench with anticipation. "Which surface first?"

Josh gave me a wicked grin. "The kitchen island."

I stood up and quickly began stripping out of my clothes. I didn't have any fear of the kids waking up with as much as they played today. Josh stood up, and before I knew it, he was naked and picking me up. He carried me into our new kitchen and then placed me on the cold stone counter. I let out a gasp. He crawled up, and I lay down as he spread my legs open to him with his knee. The smile he gave me caused me to smile even bigger. He pushed into me, and I let out a moan. When he pulled out, I gave him a look.

"Hey." I jutted out my lower lip and pouted.

"Turn around, baby, and hold on to the edge of the counter."

I quickly moved and placed myself in position. I moaned as he pushed deeper inside me.

"Yes...feels so good," I whispered.

He grabbed on to my hips and began moving in and out of me, fast and hard. I dropped my head and pushed back each time he pushed into me. I needed it deeper. I needed him to hit that one spot that would push me over the edge.

Josh was moaning, and he kept repeating how good I felt. "Damn...Heather, baby, I'm so close."

I pushed back harder, and it hit the spot. I sprang my eyes open, and I was about to tell him I was close when I saw Libby sitting on the kitchen floor, looking up at me.

Oh. My. God.

"Josh!"

"Yeah, baby, feels so good. You want it harder?"

"Josh! Josh! Josh! Stop!"

"Mmm...oh yeah, baby—wait, what? Stop?"

I used my hand and began swatting back at him. "Stop! Libby! Libby is sitting here on the floor, looking up at me!"

"What?"

Josh pulled out of me so fast, and he jumped off the island. He ran into the laundry room, and the next thing I knew, he was running out with a towel wrapped around him. He handed me one, and I carefully wrapped it around me before getting off the island.

Josh bent down and said, "Hey, baby girl. What are you doing down here?"

"There was a butterfly flying in my room, and I followed it down here."

Josh looked at me, and I shrugged.

"Baby, you can't get up and walk around the house at night. This new house is way too big."

She shrugged her shoulders and looked at us.

"Sleepwalking again?" I asked.

Josh carefully picked her up, and she snuggled into his chest. My own butterflies took off in my stomach, just like they did every time I saw Josh holding our daughter. I loved seeing her so safe in his arms.

We walked back up the stairs, and Josh placed a sleeping Libby into her bed. We stood there for a few minutes, just watching her. Josh motioned for us to leave. I carefully shut the door and then followed Josh into Will's room. I had been pleasantly surprised that neither one of them threw a fit about not sleeping in the same room. I was hoping it hadn't been because they were so tired and just hadn't felt like it, but rather, they were ready to separate a little from one another.

Josh and I quietly made our way back to the living room. We gathered our clothes and headed to our bedroom. We walked in, and I shut the door before we both busted out laughing. I fell onto the bed and held my stomach as I laughed my ass off.

"I opened my eyes, and there she was, just sitting on the floor and looking up at me!"

Josh was chortling so hard that he could hardly breathe. "Oh my gosh. These two kids are going to be a damn handful. What are we going to do about her sleepwalking?"

I sat up and took a deep breath as I wiped my tears away. "I guess we'll have to get a little alarm on her door, like the doctor suggested. I really think it has to do with the separate bedrooms."

"I agree. It seems like this all started after we talked to them about it."

I let out a sigh and turned to him. "Baby, I'm exhausted."

He pulled my towel off and gently laid me back on the bed. He kissed me so gently and tenderly that I instantly relaxed. We both crawled under the covers as Josh pulled me up against him.

"You know, I wouldn't trade any of it, not a damn thing."

I smiled and thought about how we had already made some wonderful memories in just one day. "I wouldn't either."

I listened as Josh's breathing slowed, and he drifted off to sleep. It didn't take long before I closed my eyes and dreamed of chasing butterflies.

Chapter Ten

Josh

HEATHER HANDED ME a beer as she sat down next to me. We watched as Will and Libby played with the new puppy.

"Not even two days, Josh."

"What? They needed a puppy."

Heather laughed. "They did not need a puppy this soon. Now, we have two three-year-olds and a ten-week-old chocolate lab."

I chuckled as I watched Boo chase after Libby. "I still can't believe Will let Libby name the puppy."

"I know. He has such a sweet and tender heart when it comes to Libby."

"I feel sorry for any boy who falls in love with her. He will not only have to deal with me, but he'll also have to deal with her brother."

We sat in silence for a few minutes and took our surroundings all in. The rest of the gang was planning on coming over for dinner tonight. They'd planned to bring all the side dishes, and we were going to grill up hamburgers and hot dogs.

"Just having everyone right down the road is going to be so nice. I do feel bad for Brad and Amanda though," I said.

I waited for Heather to respond. When she didn't, I glanced over to her. I quickly got up and fell down onto my knees in front of her. She was sitting there, crying.

"Baby, what's wrong? Heather?"

I looked behind me to see where she was staring. Will and Libby were sitting on the ground with Boo, so I knew they were okay.

I turned back to Heather and placed my hands on her face. "Heather? Baby, please tell me why you're upset."

She shook her head and smiled. "I'm not upset. I'm happy."

I frowned as I tilted my head, and I used my finger to make her look at me. "You're crying because you're happy?"

She smiled big and nodded her head. She glanced up and over my shoulder, and then she looked back into my eyes. "I feel them here with us."

"Your parents?"

"Yes." She let out a sob and glanced back out into the distance.

When I turned again to see what she was looking at, I saw it. "Oh, wow," I whispered. "He is huge."

I stood up and looked at the buck that was standing there, looking in our direction. He had to be at least a twelve point.

Heather stood up next to me and took my hand in hers. "Nothing but good things are going to happen here. Our kids are going to grow up in the country with their friends. They're going to swing off rope swings into the river, riding horses, and having parties in the hay fields. They're going to fall in love and come back to this house. Then, our family will grow bigger. It's going to be perfect, Josh."

I nodded my head and watched as the buck turned and began walking toward the tree line.

He stopped just short of it and turned back. *Take care of my Princess.*

A tear slowly moved down my face as I whispered, "I will."

The buck walked into the trees right as Libby and Will came running up. I bent down, and Libby tackle-hugged me.

"Daddy! I wuv you!"

"I love you, too, Libby."

Will smiled at me and then took off running again. I barely stood up and made it back to my chair. My knees felt weak. Heather leaned against the post as she gave me the most beautiful smile.

"I love you, Heather."

"I love you more," she said.

I glanced out at Libby and Will and then looked back at Heather. *We were going to be happy here.* The memories had already begun.

I smiled at Heather and motioned for her to come and sit down on my lap. She sat and raised her eyebrow as she wiggled on top of me.

I pressed my lips to her neck and moved them up to her ear. I whispered, "I love you more...plus infinity. I will forever be faithful to our love."

The End

Connect

Kelly's Facebook Page
www.facebook.com/kellyelliottauthor

Kelly's Amazon Author Page
https://goo.gl/RGVXqv

Follow Kelly on Instagram
www.instagram.com/authorkellyelliott

Follow Kelly on BookBub
www.bookbub.com/profile/kelly-elliott

Kelly's Pinterest Page
www.pinterest.com/authorkellyelliott

Kelly's Author Website
www.kellyelliottauthor.com

About the Author

Kelly Elliott is a *New York Times* and *USA Today* bestselling contemporary romance author. Since finishing her bestelling Wanted series, Kelly has continued to spread her wings while remaining true to her roots with stories of hot men, strong women, and beautiful surroundings. Her bestselling works included *Wanted, Broken, Without You,* and *Lost Love.* Elliott has been passionate about writing since she was fifteen. After years of filling journals with stories, she finally followed her dream and published her first novel, Wanted, in November 2012.

Elliott lives in Central Texas with her husband, daughter, and two pups. When she's not writing, she enjoys reading and spending time with her family. She is down to earth and very in touch with her readers, both on social media and at signings. To learn more about Kelly and her books, you can find her through her website, www.kellyelliottauthor.com.